Faces in the Crowd

Faces in the Crowd

Encounters with Jesus

Sylvia Bunting

© Sylvia Bunting, 2012

Published by Ortolan Press

A CIP catalogue record for this book is available from the British Library.

ISBN 978-0-9571172-0-4

Book and cover design by Clare Brayshaw

Prepared and printed by:

York Publishing Services Ltd
64 Hallfield Road
Layerthorpe
York YO31 7ZQ

Tel: 01904 431213

Website: www.yps-publishing.co.uk

To John

who has been there all the way

Contents

Acknowledgements

I would like to thank:

Clare, Duncan and everyone at York Publishing Services whose help and expertise turned the spoken word into the published word.

Kat, Alison and Catherine
whose penetrating encouragement as fellow-writers
has been an ongoing spur and support.

The congregations in York and Wantage
whose worship first offered a home for these reflections.

Foreword

When a royal event such as a coronation or a marriage takes place, the TV coverage is wide-ranging.

First we see the set pieces, carefully staged interviews with the principal characters.

Then comes the hoofbeat-by-heartbeat commentary as events unroll.

But in the intervals, the microphone and camera go walkabout, accosting some of the thousands thronging the way.

For a few seconds we hear the experiences of unknown people: how far they have travelled, what this event means to them and their families, how a famous face smiled and waved just for them.

They are more than devices to fill time: we see reflected on their faces the excitement of this contact with royalty; as we share their journey we hear new aspects of the epic event.

They are part of the story.

They are the faces in the crowd.

Part I

Say Yes to the Angel

Nathan 1

∗ 1 ∗

What really bugged Nathan was having to sleep in the shed. It was the last straw. As if he hadn't had more than his share of hard luck anyway. Somehow he felt he could cope with the really big things – losing his parents, being separated from Abi and Josh, having to work in this scruffy inn; but what most bugged him was that he hadn't even a decent place to sleep.

Often at night he would lie awake, thinking back over the last twelve months. It seemed light years away, the time when they had been happy at home together. For some reason he blamed Abi for starting it all. If she hadn't got married and left them, the other disasters might not have happened.

It seemed like only a few days after the wedding that his father had fallen ill. Nathan hadn't paid much attention at first, going off with his friends to get out of the house, waiting for his dad to recover. But his father hadn't recovered. Nathan had come home one day to the sound of wailing. All the neighbours had come to join his mother in mourning. His father was dead. Abi had come home for a few days, leaving Gideon to fend for himself. His mother had hugged them all close and had said through her tears 'We're still a family. We'll look after each other. In a few years Nathan will be old enough to get a job, and until then we'll manage.'

Nathan had swelled with pride at the prospect of being the man of the family, but none of it happened. The day after they buried his father, his mother fell ill. Nathan stuck by her side, barely leaving her for a moment, but it was no use. When his mother died, Nathan had shouted at Abi 'It's all your fault. If you'd looked after her properly she wouldn't have died'. Abi had tried to hug him, but he had shrugged her off while Josh looked on in wide-eyed silence.

Things went from bad to worse. He and Josh had moved in with Abi and Gideon, but Gideon was too bossy to live with. Nathan remembered shouting at him once 'I haven't got to do what you say. You're not my father.' He was not surprised when Gideon found him a job to get him out of the way. Josh had stayed, of course. Josh hardly said a word, but he wouldn't let Abi or Gideon out of his sight. In the end Gideon had said, 'He can come out in the fields with me and the others. A lad comes in handy with sheep, and he can learn the work slowly.'

So Josh would have a proper job as a shepherd, while Nathan was at everyone's beck and call. Waiting on travellers, cleaning up after them, looking after their animals, running errands for Jonas and Sarah... and sleeping in the shed.

Jonas called it a stable, but really it was only a lean-to shed at the back of the inn. Their own cow and donkey lived there, and any guests' animals. Mainly donkeys. Sometimes a horse if a Roman stopped briefly at the inn. Occasionally a camel if they had really exotic travellers, but not many of those came to Bethlehem.

Nathan was actually quite comfortable. He had made himself a den of straw, on a high platform behind the manger, that went back a long way under the angle of the roof. Abi had given him a blanket, and he had pinched a mug and a plate from her house, that used to be his mother's. He thought she hadn't noticed. He kept them safe there, out of sight at the back.

He had taken a stack of the animals' straw, which Jonas said he could have. He had also taken quite a lot of hay, a bit at a time. He wasn't supposed to have that, because the animals needed it for fodder, but it was softer than straw, and smelt better. And Nathan thought he was worth more than any old donkeys, even if he was treated like one.

In fact, although he didn't realise it, Nathan acted like a donkey. Stubborn and unhelpful.

'Nathan, fetch these things from the market.'

'Must I?'

'Nathan, take the men their meal and bring back the dirty plates.'

'Huh'.

'Nathan, shake out these blankets for me'

'Can't someone else do it?'

He refused things so often that Sarah once said he should have been called 'No-than'.

But once in a while it was useful to be able to say no. For the first time Jonas had recognised his skills.

'Nathan, if anyone else comes to the door, go and tell them we've no room. Not for anyone, under any circumstances. No matter how much they offer to pay. I haven't got room tonight for Caesar himself, though I wouldn't mind telling him how much trouble he's caused.'

Caesar had decided to hold a census. Nathan did not know the ins and outs of it, but apparently everyone had to go to their ancestors' home and be counted, so that Caesar knew how many subjects he had in his empire.

At first Nathan thought that everyone in Judea had to come to Bethlehem, but Sarah had told him no, not everyone, just the ones descended from King David's father, Jesse, who had lived in Bethlehem 400 years ago.

Even with just these, the town was bursting at the seams. By mid-afternoon every corner of floor space at the inn was occupied, and people kept on coming. Nathan quite enjoyed being allowed to say no for once.

'No room here.'

'But the other inns are full too. Where can we go?'

'Sorry, can't help you.'

No-one could get past him. He had turned down lavish bribes and stood his ground against a couple of serious heavies. But the weary young couple who came late in the evening didn't try either. When he said 'no room' they seemed to sag in despair and didn't move for a minute. The girl clung on to her donkey a bit tighter – she looked tired enough to fall off. She reminded Nathan a bit of Abigail, but Abi's baby wasn't due for another two months, and this girl looked as if her baby could arrive any minute.

Perhaps drawn by Nathan's silence, Jonas spoke over his shoulder, 'No room... I'm very sorry.' The last words were added as he saw the girl's condition.

Encouraged by the undoubted sympathy, the young man took half a step forward.

'Isn't there anywhere at all? Even a haystack would be better than the open.'

In spite of himself Nathan scanned the crowded room, but there wasn't enough room for a pigeon, let alone for these two. Then, as he turned back to the couple, he heard Jonas saying slowly,

'The only thing... there is the stable. That's pretty full too, but you could push the beasts a bit closer together. It might be better than nothing.'

Nathan was furious. His place, his own private place, being offered to someone else just like that. But he need not have worried. Even as he looked, the young man drew himself up.

'Thank you very much,' he said stiffly, 'but I don't think ...'

He was interrupted as the girl pulled his sleeve. She murmured something Nathan couldn't quite hear. It sounded like 'Say yes to the angel' but Nathan knew that neither he nor Jonas were angels.

He certainly did not feel angelic as at Jonas' bidding he took the young couple round to the shed. As he opened the door the smell of the beasts crowded into the little place staggered even him for a moment. But he went on in and said ungraciously,

'Well, here it is. It's like he said – not much.'

The young woman slid off the donkey with a sigh of relief, but the young man was looking keenly at Nathan.

'Something's the matter' he said slowly. 'Is this your place?' Resentfully Nathan nodded.

The man went down on one knee so that he could look at Nathan eye to eye.

'I'm sorry' he said earnestly, 'but I must get Mary under a roof of some kind. You can see how she is. We won't trouble you any more than we can help. Please may we stay?'

It was the first time for a year that anyone had asked Nathan for a kindness. He choked for a moment, then nodded.

The man stuck his hand out. 'Thanks... ??' Nathan shook the hand and said gruffly,

'I'm Nathan.'

'And I'm Joseph' came the reply.

* 2 *

Nathan had to scoot back to the inn in answer to a loud summons, but an hour later the work eased and he slipped back to the shed to see how they were. He found that

Joseph had cleared a space at the far end, and had swept the floor – a very necessary job. He had scraped together a small pile of straw and Mary was sitting on it, leaning back against the wall with her eyes closed.

Joseph was sitting on the bare mud floor. He looked up and smiled as Nathan came in. 'I hope we haven't pinched your bedspace?'

Nathan smiled back and shook his head. 'I have the shelf up there, but you wouldn't fit on it.'

He looked again at Joseph's arrangements, then put one foot on the edge of the empty, rickety manger and swung up to his den. Without another word he took an armful of clean straw, wriggled to the edge and threw it down to Joseph. Then he returned for another armful and another. Mary opened her eyes at the sound of movement and as she saw the air full of moving gold she laughed in delight.

Joseph piled the straw into a deep, comfortable bed for Mary, and was about to spread his cloak on top of it when Nathan called,

'Hang on a minute,' and then vaulted down carrying a soft brown blanket. 'You'll need your cloak yourself,' he said gruffly, and shot off back to his work.

When he finally finished it was late. He came back to the stable quietly, carrying the jug of wine and the bowl of stew Sarah had sent. This time Joseph did not look up. His attention was fixed on Mary. As Nathan cautiously approached he saw that her baby had been born. Tired but glowing, Mary was just wrapping the baby in the tight swaddling clothes which would help him feel safe and secure in the wide new world.

Nathan remembered that when Josh was born they had put him in a cradle. That was the proper thing to do. He looked round helplessly for anything that might serve, but all he could see was the empty manger. The donkeys had taken the last wisp of visible hay, and the bare slats were neither safe nor comfortable for a baby. But Nathan felt that he was the host. It was up to him to provide something.

Stifling a sigh, he swung up to his den via his usual foothold on the manger side. But it felt different and he hung over the edge of his shelf to look. Two of the ribs had always been rotten and unsafe – it would have been a dangerous step for anyone less agile than Nathan. But the rotten slats had been replaced by firm, new ones. He looked at Joseph in amazement. Joseph caught his eye and laughed.

'I'm a carpenter,' he said, 'and most of my tools travel with me. It is a small return for your hospitality.'

Nathan couldn't think of a reply, so he dived back to the remnants of his den. He had planned to save the hay for his own bed, but now he scooped it up and dropped it carefully into the manger.

Swinging down again he said 'I thought that might make it comfortable for the baby.'

* 3 *

It was much later in the night, and Mary was asleep. Nathan looked over the edge of his bed shelf and found Joseph wide awake. With a jerk of his head Joseph invited Nathan down.

Nathan did not need a second invitation. And he knew how to begin the conversation. He had heard the polite opening query times beyond number in the inn.

'Have you come far?' he asked.

'From Nazareth in Galilee,' Joseph answered.

It was like talking to a big brother. Nathan was soon deep in conversation, finding out about Joseph and for the first time sharing his own life story. It was good to talk, and the time passed rapidly. Eventually Nathan put the question which had been buzzing in his mind all night.

'When Jonas offered you the place here' he asked, 'and you were going to turn it down' (Joseph grinned) 'Mary said something that changed your mind. What was it she said?'

Joseph's eyes changed focus, as if he were looking at something a long way away. 'Mmm, yes' he answered. 'She said, 'Say yes to the angel'.'

Nathan was puzzled.

'But there weren't any angels there' he said. 'What did she mean? And how did you understand what she meant?'

Joseph leaned back against the wall. 'It's a long story' he said.

'When Mary and I got engaged, life was brilliant. I felt as if the future had an archway saying 'happy ever after' and we were both so happy. Then Mary told me that she was pregnant.'

Nathan stirred in surprise. Joseph had not seemed that sort of person. Joseph caught his thought and shook his head.

'No, he wasn't mine. He wasn't any other man's either. Mary told me that this was something to do with God, and that an angel had spoken to her about it. She had said yes.'

Nathan's face was screwed up in perplexity and disbelief. Joseph looked at him and continued,

'Yes, I thought pretty well what you're thinking. But I didn't want to make matters any worse for Mary. I was still trying to decide what to do when the angel spoke to me.'

Nathan shot bolt upright.

'You mean you've seen an angel? Like our ancestor Jacob and the prophet Isaiah?'

Joseph grinned. 'Remember Balaam the prophet? His donkey saw an angel too. That's more my level.'

'What was the angel like? What did he say?' It never occurred to Nathan to disbelieve Joseph. Truth writes itself on the heart.

'What was he like?' Joseph reflected. 'Like a dream, in a way, where the most preposterous things happen but you accept them. He was immense, but very compact. Like all the power in the world compressed into a box. And he was so alive and so full of joy. But frightening, too, because you knew that if you listened to him life would be totally different afterwards.'

'Surely you had to listen to him? You can't ignore an angel' Nathan was definite.

'That's the crucial thing. You don't have to listen, and you don't have to go along with what he says. Angels always leave you a choice; God always leaves you a choice.'

Nathan was struggling to understand. 'You mean, like when you came in here and asked me if you could stay? And left it to me to decide?'

'That's exactly it' Joseph nodded. 'Once you realise that's how God treats us, you can't really go cracking the whip on other people.'

'Not even if you know you're right?'

'Especially if you know you're right.'

Nathan moved on 'But what did he say?'

'That the child is God's son, and is to be the Messiah. And he wants me to look after Mary.'

Nathan was gobsmacked. He gazed at Joseph without speaking and saw that Joseph was looking protectively at Mary and at the baby, both peacefully sleeping.

Joseph's eyes returned to Nathan.

'We shall call him Jesus, but his other name is Emmanuel.'

Nathan worked it out slowly, 'That means... God with us'. Joseph nodded. Nathan was out of his depth. He looked at the baby – so ordinary. If he was God's son, shouldn't there be more fuss than this? He returned to what he could understand.

'And what did you say to the angel?'

Joseph looked straight at him. 'I think you know what I said.'

'You said yes'.

Joseph nodded again. 'When Mary and I talked it over, we both felt totally scared, but totally sure we wanted to go along with God. It became a watchword between us; that however God spoke to us we would say yes.'

'Has he talked to you since?'

'Yes, but in different ways. Often through circumstances, like the stable tonight. That's what Mary meant.'

Nathan drew a deep breath. 'Does that mean that sometimes when we say no to other people we're saying no to God?'

'Sometimes' Joseph said quietly. He had heard a lot about Nathan that night.

They fell into a friendly silence. The candle flickered in the lantern. Mary and the baby slept.

Suddenly there was a loud grating sound. Someone was slowly pushing open the door on its rusty hinges. In a flash Joseph and Nathan were on their feet. Nathan pounded to the door. To his amazement it was Josh, wildly out of breath.

'I thought you were out in the fields tonight' Nathan told his brother.

Josh nodded and came in, closing the door behind him.

'I am. We were... But suddenly – there was an angel.' He looked warily at Nathan as if he did not expect to be believed, but Nathan just nodded and asked 'What did he say?'

'That he brought great news, for us to tell everyone else. That the Messiah has been born here in Bethlehem. And then it wasn't just one but hundreds of angels, as if heaven had moved into our field.'

'And what did you say?' Nathan asked intently.

'You don't say much to a sky full of angels. But after they'd gone, everyone started talking about whether to come and look for the Messiah. We wanted to, but... where do you start in a town this size? So they decided to send me to ask you and Abi if you'd heard anything. But the odd thing is, they said he'd be lying in a manger.'

Nathan nodded and moved aside.

'That's right' he said, 'in my manger.' For the first time Josh could see the far end of the stable; Mary and Joseph close together, and the baby with his eyes wide open.

The brothers walked up the stable together to the manger. Josh drew a deep breath.

'Wow' he said. Then after a few moments, 'I must tell the others.'

'Yes' Nathan took his arm and shook it urgently. 'Tell them to come. Tell them to say yes to the angel.'

The Soldier

Marcus lied about his age to get into the army. His mother lied too, but that was not unusual. The magistrate had looked at Marcus with as much expression as a dead haddock on a fishmonger's slab.

'Well, young man? Anything to say? Any reason why I shouldn't send you down for a few years?' His clerk had leaned forward and muttered something. 'My clerk reminds me that you could opt for army service as an alternative, but I doubt if you're old enough. How old are you?'

'Sixteen, your worship'. Marcus's answer came out as promptly as if it were the truth. He stood tall and stared defiantly at the magistrate. The man frowned, sensing something wrong.

'Can anyone confirm that? Are this boy's parents in court?' Rising to her moment of glory, Julia stepped out of the crowd. She smoothed her clothes and put on her most deferential smile. No-one pointed out the splashes down her front that looked like spilt soup.

'Sadly, he's my son, your Lordship. Everything that you've heard about him is true, but I'm only a poor widow with five other children, and try as I could, this lad got into bad company. I'd be glad for him to go into the army. The discipline could be the making of him, and service overseas would do him good.'

Marcus heard the unspoken subtitles. Service overseas would get him out of her hair, with no danger of him punching the next man she brought home. And in the army he might even get killed. He was not surprised when she declared that he was sixteen, and waited for her to add 'Of course, I was very young when he was born'.

The dead haddock did not blink, just turned back to Marcus. 'Very well. Theft and grievous bodily harm. Six years army service, no remission. Next case?'

From there on Marcus never stood still. He was passed from one person to another, one place to the next, a human baton in the military relay. He learned to clean his uniform, use his weapons, drill relentlessly and salute anything that moved.

By the end of the process, he passed out near the top of his group, almost in the running for the sword of honour. Marcus waited eagerly for the announcement of his first posting. They said Germany was good, with a decent social life.

It wasn't Germany, it was the Middle East. Marcus scowled. Any empire was bound to have its trouble spots, but this was the pits. He went in search of his friend Titus, a veteran who had been there, seen it, done it all. But all he had for Marcus was one caution: 'Be careful of anyone in flowing robes, Jew or Arab. They can hide all sorts of mischief in those robes, so look out. Sure, they hate each other, but they hate Rome worse, and the Roman army most of all.'

Then Titus stood up. 'Your first posting' he announced. 'you must do this properly. Seek the goodwill of the gods, and bid a proper farewell to your family'.

Marcus laughed. 'Would you like me to go and salute Emperor Augustus as well?' but Titus didn't smile. 'A soldier should have the gods on his side. A bit of help from up there in battle might make all the difference. Come on now – Mars or Jupiter?'

Marcus shrugged. What harm could it do? 'If you want to go god-bothering, let's make it Jupiter. He outranks them all, doesn't he? Let's go to the top.' Titus had already turned, heading for the forum. In front of the temple of Jupiter the Thunderbolt, Titus reached for his pouch, but Marcus forestalled him.

'It's OK, I've got all my pay. How much does it cost to visit this god?' Titus sorted out a few small coins from Marcus's palm. 'The priests ask for as much as you can afford, but I'll tell them you spent your money on your girlfriend.' Before Marcus could protest, they were climbing the steps to the massive temple and stood beneath Jupiter's ponderous statue. Eventually a priest in a grubby robe ambled up to them.

'We sail for Judea tomorrow, and my friend wishes to offer a sacrifice and consult the auspices.' Marcus hardly knew what Titus meant, but the priest sniffed, took the coins, and led them to an altar in a dark corner. With no ceremony he took a cockerel from a nearby pen, cut its throat and slung it onto the altar. Slitting open the bird's body, he prodded its innards with the knife blade.

'Jupiter is pleased to accept your sacrifice and the organs assure the god's blessing for a safe voyage.' The priest picked up the cockerel and shuffled off into the darkness.

Marcus felt completely flat. He hadn't known what to expect in a temple, but more than this, surely. 'What difference can that make? Jupiter wouldn't have stopped feasting long enough to notice us!' Titus shook his head sagely. 'The gods may or may not exist, but if they do, you stand a better chance if you keep in with them'. Marcus hoped he wouldn't ever be in the kind of situation where a stringy cockerel made the difference between life and death.

Then as he plodded morosely on he realised he was on familiar ground. He jerked his head at the tall tenement across the street and said to Titus, 'My mother's place'. By the time Titus had seized his elbow and marched him up the three flights of stairs, Marcus was regretting his words. He'd forgotten the stink of cabbage in the hallway, and he aimed a savage kick at a rat scuttling ahead of him.

Suddenly an ill-fitting door flew open and a boy hurtled out, squawking as his head hit Marcus's breastplate. He rebounded against the doorpost and stared at Marcus defiantly. 'Julia's out and I don't know when she'll be back, so you can't come in.' Marcus reached out and grabbed his shoulder. 'What kind of welcome is that? You idiot, Lucius, I'm Marcus!'

Emotions chased across Lucius' expression. Puzzlement, a delighted smile, then caution and a closed face. 'Hello Marcus. You can't come back, I've got your bed, and Flavian gave me your place in the gang. Anyway, you're too posh for us now.' He stood blocking the doorway, but flinched as Marcus moved.

'Don't worry' Marcus fished in his pouch. 'Here, get something to eat, and share it with the others.' He turned away as Lucius grabbed the coins, but Titus stooped down. His voice was unexpectedly gentle. 'Hey, lad, just tell me how old you are, you and your brother'. Lucius considered, but couldn't see any harm in it. 'I'm twelve, and Marcus is thirteen.' As Titus stood up, the boy darted inside and slammed the door.

Halfway back to barracks, Marcus found his voice. 'Are you going to report me, then, for being under age?' Titus shook his head. 'I reckon the army is your best hope now. Let's trust that cockerel works'.

As he set sail next morning Marcus didn't bother looking either at the seafarers' shrine or the small crowd waving on the quayside. Gods or human beings, no-one would be there for him.

Judea was empty. No-one around, apart from a few distant figures tilling the brown fields. Even the scattered villages looked uninhabited.

'Where – are the – natives?' he asked Titus, out of breath at the steep pace uphill. His friend grinned.

'You're out in the colonies now. If you can catch a local, you can make him carry your pack for a mile. They go underground at the first sound of troops on the road.'

Marcus could understand that. His pack straps were wearing grooves in his shoulders, and no-one in his senses would volunteer for a load like this. He eased the straps again and looked forward to a rest in the barracks in Jerusalem.

But they had barely arrived when the whole garrison was called on parade. Caesar Augustus had decreed military support for the forthcoming census of his subjects. An army presence was necessary at each census point. Detachments would leave tomorrow.

Marcus was disgusted. 'Not even a day to see the sights before we have to go and nurse some pen-pusher. Why do they need us? Can't the civil service do its own counting?'

Titus knew all about it, of course. 'This country's a bad place for a census. One of their kings took a census a few centuries back, and their god sent a plague to punish him for presumption. No way will they cooperate now.' With a history like that, Marcus was amazed the detachments were so small. Only two soldiers per village, but at least the centurion had put him with Titus. They would set off at dawn.

He dumped his pack in his bed-space and looked round. Most of the others were asking the way to local bars, but you could drink at any old time. 'Isn't there anything worth looking at in this place?'

Titus sighed. 'Not unless you're into temples.'

Marcus was cautious. 'How many temples? How big?'

'Oh, only one. They only allow one god here.' But the temple was definitely big, with an atmosphere you could almost touch. Then Marcus stopped looking at the building and watched the people. Everyone avoided the soldiers, but he could still see their faces. As they went in they looked keyed up, almost excited. And coming out they looked different: uplifted somehow, and satisfied.

'I want to go in' he said suddenly, and without waiting he plunged through the crowded gateway. Titus' hand fell on his shoulder. 'One warning. Don't go any further than this courtyard, or they'll kill you. I mean it.' Before Marcus could query this, he saw a stall selling pigeons. Fishing for a few coins, he stalked up to the seller. 'I'll have a pigeon, and make it a fat one – I don't go in for mingy sacrifices.'

'You – you want to offer a sacrifice?' the seller looked more hostile than pleased.

'Why not?' Marcus asked, 'One god is as good as the next.' Marcus could feel a crowd gathering behind him. He suddenly felt very conspicuous in his uniform. Instinctively his hand went to his sword. The stall-holder stiffened, and gulped. Marcus was sourly pleased that the man was nervous, but could not believe what he heard. 'I'm sorry, I can't sell you a bird. You can't make a sacrifice here.'

Marcus almost snarled. 'You should be pleased I want to honour your god. In Rome the gods accept sacrifices from all who come.' The man gulped again, and left it to his neighbour to say 'The Lord only accepts sacrifices from his own people. We can't sell you anything.'

A Jewish tradesman refusing to sell to a customer! Marcus would have laughed if the atmosphere had not been so threatening. Pressure on his shoulder blades told him that Titus had moved to stand back to back with him.

The muttering in the crowd suddenly stopped. The soldiers braced themselves for an onslaught.

But the new voice was quiet and peaceable. 'What is the trouble?' The stallholders competed in a tangle of explanation, but the man seemed to grasp it all very quickly. Old, Marcus thought. He sounds old, but they respect him. Then the newcomer moved into his line of sight. He smiled and nodded. 'Yes,' he said, 'things are difficult at the moment. Only those who become Jews are able to worship the One True God.'

The gentleness of his speech robbed his words of arrogance, and he smiled at Marcus like an equal. 'God has chosen the Jews to know him in a special way, you see.' Marcus shook his head to clear it. 'You mean people can get to know your God?' he asked in disbelief.

The man nodded. 'God wants all his children to know him, and to love him as he loves them. One day the whole world will be included, but for now we're still waiting for God's final step towards us.'

Marcus pulled a face. He knew how little love there was in the world. The man was barking mad. Which was a shame because he looked a decent, sensible type. No point in arguing with him though.

The old man smiled, almost as if he'd read Marcus' mind. 'Oh yes, it will happen. In my lifetime too. God's glory will blaze out from Israel to every nation in the world.' Surprisingly, the crowd behind Marcus sounded as disconcerted as he was. There were whispers and mutterings, and Marcus had the strong feeling that this man was one on his own. The speaker's eyes ranged over the crowd and his voice deepened. 'Many Jews will find him a stumbling block, but those who fall can be restored. And God's sword will pierce more sharply than any Roman weapon.'

Marcus's hand jerked away from his own sword. He wanted to ask more, but Titus' grip on his elbow was urgent. He took a step towards the gate, then turned back. 'Who are you, sir? Are you a priest?'

'No, but God speaks to everyone who lives close to him. My name is Simeon.'

Marcus was dragged away before he could answer, and as they went down the hill he blocked the man's peculiar forecast from his mind. His own future was definite, and he'd better concentrate on it. 'How far to march tomorrow?' he asked, 'to this census place?'

Titus sounded relieved to be back on military ground. 'Six miles, due south,' he answered. 'a village called Bethlehem.'

3

Bethlehem deafened Marcus. The noise of hundreds of people echoed in the narrow lanes, and even their uniform did not prevent them being knocked and buffeted as they forced their way towards the market square.

'I hadn't expected it to be so busy' Marcus said in surprise.

'This is where their King David was born. Half the families in Judea claim descent from him.'

There wasn't anything very kingly about the crowds jostling them. The two soldiers headed for the census table and with a clashing of arms took up a position one on each side. Marcus caught his breath as he gazed over the horde of hostile, bearded faces.

But as the hours went by he became interested in the crowd, some of them sitting picnicking as they waited. He would welcome a swig from his own wine flask, but wasn't sure if it was a good idea to show such human weakness. To distract himself, he turned slightly and watched the man standing at the census table.

'Joseph bar Jacob bar Matthan bar Eleazar...' he was saying when the clerk slammed his hand on the table.

'Three generations is enough. I don't need your pedigree back to King Solomon. Married?'

Joseph bar Jacob nodded and indicated the woman standing close behind him.

'Chidren?' A raucous laugh went up from the men around, and one wit yelled out 'Ask him again tomorrow!' Marcus saw that Joseph's wife was heavily pregnant. The clerk was waving them away. They stopped for a moment almost touching Marcus, and the woman's tired face looked close to tears.

'Get her back to your inn,' Marcus said quickly to Joseph. 'Are you staying nearby?'

The Judean shrugged. 'Not as yet. We thought we'd better sign in first, then Mary can rest.' Mary hung on to his arm and they moved heavily off through the crowd. Marcus hoped they found somewhere soon, then remembered that he and Titus hadn't anywhere to stay yet either. It didn't matter – Titus would find them a billet.

At the thought his eyes went to his friend, still unmoved at attention. But just as he looked, Titus staggered. This was unknown – Titus was always the steadiest soldier on parade. Marcus whirled round further and saw a thin trickle of red trickling down his friend's armour, from the small area where his neck was unprotected. At the same time a brown-clad Jew came sliding round the back of the table. Marcus reached out instinctively and grabbed him.

Titus swayed and gently collapsed into a heap. The clerks sat open-mouthed and looked at Marcus for instructions. He had never felt more alone.

Desperately he struggled not to show weakness or hesitation. A woman to take Titus to her home. Men to carry him there. More men to take the prisoner to the magistrate. Witnesses...

At that point the crowd grew rapidly thinner, all holding out empty hands and protesting they had seen nothing. Before his sizzling anger could erupt, a lad his own age stepped forward. 'I saw that man stab the other soldier. I'll say so.'

Marcus heard muffled chuckles, and knew something wasn't right. Glaring at the oldest man present, he asked coldly,

'What is going on here?' The beard hid a smirk, but the man's tone was polite.

'Reuben is a shepherd boy, sir. By our laws, shepherds aren't allowed to give evidence. They're not trustworthy enough'. The boy turned red but stood his ground. 'I did see it. And I will say so!'

The remaining clerk coughed. 'There is still the census…'

Marcus never remembered how he got through the rest of the day. But the worst was over, and at sunset he checked on Titus. He was conscious and being well treated, but the woman of the house was firm that Marcus couldn't stay in her house. 'A sick man, yes. A soldier in arms, no'. Marcus had been too grateful to make a fuss, which was why he was now wandering aimlessly, looking for somewhere to rest, himself. The village was like an anthill, full of bodies and no room at any of the inns.

Just as he was giving up hope, someone called. 'Sir, sir!' It was the shepherd boy. Perhaps he was too young to feel either the hostility or the fear of his countrymen. 'Come with me, if you like. We're out of doors tonight, but the sheep help us keep warm.'

The small group of shepherds welcomed him with raised eyebrows but no comments. The oldest looked Marcus up and down and said 'Shalom'. Behind him Reuben murmured 'Say Shalom too. It means peace.'

As Marcus returned the greeting, the shepherds made room round their fire and settled down for the night.

Much later, Marcus stirred on the cold ground and opened one eye. It was still dark – no need to wake up yet. All he could see was a bunch of sheep, dim grey against the night. No, not grey, more silver. Actually they were shining white in the moonlight from behind him. It was so strong now he could see his shadow stretched out on the hummocks of grass.

Was the moon as bright as this at home? He rolled over to look and was nearly blinded by the waterfall. How come he hadn't noticed that before – three times his height, with a continual flowing and splashing of foam. Funny, the shape of the rocks underneath almost made it look like a man. He could make out arms and a head, imagine piercing eyes. Not quite, though – it could perhaps be a man with wings.

The sheep scrambled to their feet and Marcus heard the shepherds grunting awake nearby. Then all sound stopped, and Marcus went rigid. The waterfall had stepped forward! It was really a person, a person made of moving light!

The sheep were all standing up, but the men were huddled to the ground. Marcus felt Reuben beside him and muttered 'Is this your God?'

Reuben's voice trembled. 'It must be one of his angels, his messengers.'

Marcus could not bear to look, but he couldn't bear not to. And the angel's eyes were looking straight at him. Then the voice spoke, like a trumpet calling reveille, but with words he could understand. 'Don't be afraid.'

Marcus saw the others moving carefully until they were sitting up – no, kneeling on the ground. Was this the end of the world? he wondered.

Then the trumpet spoke again. 'I'm bringing you good news, something to be happy about.' Marcus felt like an outsider. This was the Jews' God, speaking just to them. He leaned back, but suddenly found the angel was still looking at him. 'Not just for shepherds, not just for Jews, but for everyone in the whole world.'

'It's for everyone, but it's happening here and now, in Bethlehem, David's city. The Messiah has just been born and he will save the world. Go and see – he is wearing ordinary baby clothes, but you will recognise him because he is lying in a cattle manger.'

Suddenly the whole sky was filled with people who were light. It was like being in the middle of a stadium with the whole crowd singing. 'Glory to God, and peace for his people, the people he loves.'

It lasted for ever – or maybe for just a few minutes. When the angels had gone the shepherds were silent for a while, each gazing into space to hold on to the vision. Then one by one they moved, looked at each other, and all said the same thing, 'We must go and see this'. Marcus said it too and felt no different from the others.

The town was dark, but round one stable door shone the faint light of an oil lamp. Hesitantly Reuben pushed it, and they all crowded in. It was true. There in the manger lay a baby. Joseph bar Jacob stood nearby, and Mary lay propped on a bale of straw. They had found their night's lodging. As the men came in Mary and Joseph looked at each other and nodded slightly, as if confirming something they had never quite believed. Then Mary picked up the baby so that the visitors could see him. Her eyes caught Marcus', and she smiled in recognition.

'Shalom' she said. Marcus felt suddenly at ease, warm, welcomed.

'Shalom' he answered. For the first time in his life, he had come home.

Death in the Village

Nathan 2

* 1 *

'Food. Rest. Masters. King.' The slant-eyed boy at the inn door gazed arrogantly at Nathan. For a minute the two lads tried to stare each other down. But business was business, so Nathan gathered his store of travellers' Greek.

'Yes, we have room today. How many?'

'Four of us, and three horses, and two donkeys. We left the camels at Jericho.' A sideways glance to see if he had impressed the local boy, but Nathan did not react. He just moved to the end of the room. 'This area is the most private, and has room for four. I will put out beds'.

'No need. We have our own beds, on the pack donkey. I will put them out. My masters wish me to serve them. I understand what they require.'

Nathan shrugged. 'As you wish.' Suddenly the stranger grovelled. Dropping to his knees, he doubled over until his forehead touched the floor.

Before Nathan could take credit to himself for the change, the light from the doorway was blocked and an impatient voice spoke behind him.

'Up, Suleiman. Persian manners do not suit Judea.' Whirling round, Nathan was dazzled by vivid red and blue robes. They shimmered in the gloom – could they be silk? The effect was crowned by an elaborate turban, but the man wearing this splendour spoke simply.

24

'Has Suleiman bespoken bedspace and food? We are tired and ready for both.'

Nathan found himself bowing 'Yes, your highness. Please come in. Food will be ready immediately. I will stable your animals.' Then he hurtled into the kitchen, dimly aware that other gorgeously clad figures were entering. Beside the fire he found Sarah's friend Huldah, carrying young Jotham on her hip as always, and in full flow.

'Three kings, Sarah, they were asking at doors and I'm sure they said they were kings. They were coming this way...'

Nathan interrupted. 'They're here now. They are staying with us and want food.'

Sarah bustled into the main room, while Nathan went out to find the animals. Magnificent horses, and sleek well-fed donkeys. Suleiman was staggering under a bulky pack from one donkey, and Nathan took hold of the other end. As they carried it in, he heard the leader asking Sarah 'Where will we find the king? We are sure he is in this town.'

Sarah shook her head bemusedly. 'Not here, sir. Kings have not bothered with Bethlehem for centuries. You should go to Jerusalem.'

'We have been to Jerusalem.' The dry voice sounded as though the experience had been memorable for the wrong reasons. 'We were sent on here, I think by someone called Micah.'

Sarah frowned. 'I don't know anyone of that name. Are you sure this is the right place?'

A second traveller spoke wearily, sounding as though he had covered this subject many times before. 'This is undoubtedly a king. Born about eighteen months ago. A new star appeared at that time, and it indicated an important birth. Surely there would have been special happenings then?'

Eighteen months ago? Sarah and Nathan looked at each other. Was this another sign?

Sarah drew breath. 'Yes, there was a boy born then. He's called Jesus. His father is Joseph from Nazareth.' She would not mention the angels, Nathan knew. The whole town knew about the angels, but they never said anything to strangers.

'Where can we find him? The star led us here, but the town is a warren of streets. When we asked, no-one could help us.'

'Nathan will take you, sir, as soon as you have eaten. It is close to his sister's home.' When her brothers had poured out the story of the boy born in Nathan's stable and the shepherds seeing angels, Nathan's sister Abigail had insisted that Mary and her family came to stay with them. He thought it was because Abigail herself was pregnant – she could not bear to think of Mary without anywhere to call home. Mary was certainly a great support to Abigail when young Joe was born a few weeks later, and the two families grew together. When a house across the street fell empty, Joseph moved in with his family, but they were constantly in and out of each other's homes. Young Joe followed Jesus everywhere now they could both toddle, and both treated Nathan as their favourite uncle.

When Nathan led the splendid visitors into Mary's house, Jesus rushed to him, chuckling in delight. Joe scrambled along behind, then fell over in astonishment as he saw the tall, colourful figures. But the visitors ignored Joe, gazing eagerly at Jesus. When Nathan put him down Jesus ran to his mother, standing close and holding tightly to her skirt.

Caspar beckoned, 'Our boxes, boy.' Suleiman came forward with three inlaid boxes, and each visitor took out a key from his robes, unlocked his box, and turned back to Jesus. Then Nathan gasped. The men came forward, held out their gifts to Mary, then one by one sank to their knees in front of the child, with their foreheads to the floor as Suleiman's had been earlier. Gold glinted from one open box, and the scent of spice and incense was strong in the room.

Nathan felt awkward, almost embarrassed, like an intruder. Joe was crawling towards the strangers and reaching out to tug a gorgeous robe with one grubby hand. Nathan picked him up and went out quietly. Suleiman was standing outside. They looked at each other over Joe's head, but neither said anything for a long time.

It was late evening when Joseph came to the inn. The exotic group around the table welcomed him to a seat. The heads were too close together to hear their words, but their voices sounded sombre. Nathan caught the name Herod a couple of times, and then a discussion about the state of the roads. Joseph smiled at Nathan as he left, but did not stay to chat.

In the early hours Nathan was nudged awake. Suleiman was bending over him with a finger on his lips. 'We need the animals quietly' he murmured. Nathan realised that the Persians had packed and were dressed for departure. Caspar took coins from his belt.

'This will cover our reckoning' he said in a low voice, 'We are grateful for all you have done'. He pressed the coins into Nathan's hand. 'We need to go now while no-one can see which road we take.'

Nathan was surprised. 'Aren't you going back to Jerusalem?' he asked, 'and then Jericho...?'

'No. We shall not go back to Jerusalem.'

'But you've only just arrived. Won't you visit Mary and Jesus again?'

'A lifetime would not be long enough, but we have seen him, and we shall remember.'

Nathan brought round the animals without any further questions. He clasped hands briefly with Suleiman. 'Travel safely' he offered.

'Remain safely' answered Suleiman. It sounded an odd farewell in this peaceful village, but Nathan decided as he waved them off that it must be just one more peculiar Persian custom.

* 2 *

Nathan was still drowsy next day, when Mary called in. 'Can you stay with us tonight, Nathan? Joseph would like help with a job. I've asked Sarah and she doesn't mind.' Nathan nodded cheerfully and saluted with his broom handle as she left. Glancing up a while later he noticed Sarah still standing in the doorway, looking thoughtfully down the road.

By the time he reached Joseph's house it was dark. Joseph must be planning an early start in the morning, Nathan decided. But as he pushed the door, he saw that things were happening now. In the middle of the floor stood Joseph's work donkey, ready harnessed. Joseph was tying on the last of several bundles, and Mary was folding cloths to make a saddle. She jumped as Nathan walked in, and he thought she was trying to hold back tears.

Joseph cleared his throat gruffly. 'We couldn't go without telling you. Will you walk with us a bit of the way, and help Jesus feel everything is normal?'

Nathan's legs felt wobbly with shock. 'You're not going? Where? Why? How long?'

Mary came and put her arms round him. 'It's not safe here any longer, Nathan. The travellers told Joseph that King Herod had too much unhealthy interest in Jesus. They haven't gone back to him, but he knows about Bethlehem. We can't stay and bring danger on you all, and at all costs Jesus must be safe.'

Joseph joined them. 'I couldn't sleep last night for wondering what to do, and when I did drop off it seemed as if someone was shaking me awake and saying Egypt, Egypt – all of you.'

'Another angel?' Nathan asked.

Joseph smiled. 'Might have been, who can say? At any rate, Egypt is beyond Herod's power.'

The door opened again, silently, and Abigail slid in. She handed yet another bundle to Joseph.

'Food for the journey. It will save you having to stop where people might remember you.' Then she turned to Mary. The hug lasted for ever, and when they reluctantly let go of each other, tears were streaming down both their faces. Abi went and looked down at Jesus for a moment. 'Just keep him safe.'

She left abruptly, with a watery smile to Joseph. He sharply took hold of the donkey's bridle and tugged it toward the door. 'Pick up the child, woman. We must be on our way.'

As they trod quietly through Bethlehem Nathan talked to the drowsy child in a low voice. He could see Mary making an effort to regain her calm, and by the time they were a mile beyond the village she was able to smile at her son. Her fierce grip on him relaxed a little, but she resisted his efforts to be put down.

'Not yet, Jesus. Later. We must go faster than you can walk. But you can ride the donkey if you like'. Jesus settled happily on to the saddle cloths, with his mother's hand firmly at his back. He looked at Nathan to make sure his friend had seen his riding prowess, and chuckled as Nathan gave him a tight hug.

Nathan swallowed. 'When shall I see you again?' Mary shook her head gently. 'We don't know, Nathan. We shall never forget you. You were our first friend in Bethlehem.'

There were no more words. Nathan stood watching their figures grow steadily smaller in the distance, then dropped by the side of the road, rested his head on his knees, and wept more despairingly than them all. When he looked up again and the world came back into focus, the road was empty.

* 3 *

Next morning Jonas and Sarah made no comment on Nathan's heavy feet and heavy face. They dished out jobs as usual, and Nathan tried to work as usual, but found every movement hard. He was glad at midday, when the morning jobs were done.

As Nathan shook his last blanket in the doorway, he saw Huldah walking up the street, her head bent as she chattered to Jotham. Nathan waved to them half-heartedly and turned to go indoors.

The noise pulled him back. A jingling, clanking sound and the clump of feet tramping in unison. Then a firm command and the feet stopped sharply. Nathan peered out. Were the Romans parading through their province again?

The men were in uniform sure enough, but the armour was not Roman. These must be Jewish troops, under King Herod's personal command... Nathan's mind refocused and he watched intently.

The officer accosted Huldah with a question. Nathan watched her face take on a mask of stupidity, as she denied knowing anything about anything.

The officer turned away impatiently, with a muttered command to the nearest soldier. Huldah was quickening her step to pass when without warning the man stepped towards her and snatched Jotham away, tucking the child under one casual arm. Huldah ran after him, screaming and tugging at his arm, but two soldiers took her arms and held her there in the middle of the street, shaking and agitated. The officer looked at her again.

'You may find you remember more than you think'.

'Don't hurt him, sir, he's frightened, let me have him back. I can't tell you anything.'

The soldier held Jotham out at arm's length, gripping him by the shoulder. With his free hand he unsheathed his sword. As Huldah struggled the sword moved nearer her son.

'A fine boy. You must be proud of him. How old is he?'

'Fourteen months, sir. Please give him to me.'

'First tell me about the boy who was born here. The one who has just had some magnificent visitors. Or is this the boy we are looking for?'

Huldah writhed in the solders' grip, but was held fast. She swallowed hard. 'No, that was a different boy, sir, but I know him. I can tell you all about him if you let Jotham go.'

'Ah'. The sword was lowered and Huldah babbled hastily.

'It's Jesus you want, sir. Older than my Jotham, a few months. Kings came to see him, kings from Persia.'

Nathan winced, but the officer smiled. 'That's better. Now show me where he lives.'

He beckoned one rank of soldiers to follow him. Her escort dragged Huldah along, protesting helplessly and looking back at Jotham, still firm in the soldier's grip. As they disappeared Nathan could still hear the sound of her voice. Suddenly it stopped then started, louder than before. The group reappeared, the soldiers still dragging Huldah and the officer with an ugly look on his face. He motioned to the soldier holding Jotham. The sword rose again.

'Please don't hurt him sir. I've told you everything I know. I swear I didn't know they'd gone. Please give him back to me.'

'All right.' Huldah fell silent with relief. The officer nodded at Jotham's custodian, who drew back his sword and then thrust it expertly into the child's chest. After one convulsion Jotham was still. The soldier pulled out his sword, wiped it on the child's clothing and threw his body on the ground. The officer signed to the others to release Huldah.

'There he is. You can have him back now.'

Frozen in the doorway, Nathan realised Jonas was standing behind him, one arm round Sarah who was weeping silently into his shoulder. He noticed that other doors had been quietly closed, and did not blame the occupants. Someone would help Huldah, but not yet.

The officer was moving along the ranks, dividing the men into groups of eight. Were they going to search the town? Nathan felt immense relief that Joseph had taken his family away in time. But he couldn't take his eyes from Jotham's body. How would Mary feel if she knew someone else's child had been killed? His tumbling thought stopped as the squads moved off.

One squad stayed. Two men to each end of the street, where they stood guard. The two remaining pairs took one side of the street each. Approaching the first door quietly, one soldier flung it open abruptly and took cover against the wall outside. The other waited a moment, then ran alertly through the open door. Nathan realised they had all drawn their swords.

A moment's silence was followed by anguished screams. A girl ran out of the doorway, crying and screaming as wailing filled the house behind her.

'They've hurt James! He's all over blood and he won't move.'

The soldiers emerged with swords dripping red, and without a glance moved to the next house. The procedure was repeated and after a dreadful pause the screams broke out again. By now two soldiers had reached the inn. Nathan shrank back as the men thrust their way in.

'Who are you looking for?' Jonas' voice was almost level. 'We have no-one staying today.'

'We'll check that for ourselves.' The search went into every corner, every box and bag small enough for a child to hide. When the ransack was complete the soldiers left. The younger one nodded at Sarah. 'Be glad your children are grown.'

'Are you killing all the children?'

'Oh no. Just the boys, and then only under two'.

Joe! Nathan desperately wrenched away from Jonas and had darted half way up the street before anyone else moved. He zigzagged through a couple of alleys to the end of his own street. He was too late.

The men on guard held him back, though he struggled and battered at them, and shouted at the top of his voice,

'Abi! Get away!' It was no good. He had to watch helplessly as the soldiers repeated the deadly ritual at each house. Door. Wait. Enter. Screams. One woman ran out carrying a baby, but the soldiers waylaid her and in a moment she was holding only a small bloodstained bundle. Nathan wanted to stop his ears against the noise. The soldiers were silent but the whole town was screaming.

When they released him it was all over. Nathan stood rooted. Where was there to go? What good was anything now? What could he say to Abi? He heard a different noise, and in a gap between two houses saw another soldier. He was bent over against a wall, being sick. As he straightened he caught Nathan's eye.

'It was our orders, see? That's what a squaddie has to

do. Not think. Just obey orders.' He was almost pleading, but Nathan turned away.

As he entered the house Abi ran at him, shaking him until he staggered.

'This is all your fault. If you hadn't made friends with Joseph they'd never have stayed. I wish I'd never met them. I wish your God would leave us all alone. Ohhh' and she had thrown herself on Joe's inert body, picking him up and cradling him, murmuring baby talk until the blood seeped through her clothes too and she began weeping again.

Gideon flung the door open.

'What's happened? We heard the noise, even from the pastures. Has there been an accident? TELL ME WHAT HAS HAPPENED!'

Neither of them could find words. Neither of them could even think words. Gideon had to work it out for himself. When he did, he picked up Abi and Joe bodily, and turned on Nathan in a rage.

'Don't tell me, this has got something to do with Jesus. I knew no good would come of it. Why my son? What price your angels now?'

* 4 *

Trade dropped off at the inn, of course. Travellers were uneasy in this town full of despair and sullen hostility. Word went round – Bethlehem is under a curse, best avoid it.

This meant less work for Nathan, but that didn't help. At least when he was busy he didn't have to think about anything. One evening when they had only two travellers, Sarah flapped at him with her apron.

'Get out of here for goodness' sake! Go breathe some fresh air and find someone else to scowl at.'

He slouched into Abi's house, and found Gideon and Josh there too. Lambing must be over, then. Josh looked up hopefully at his brother's arrival, but got little response. With a small sigh he picked up his sleeping blanket, took it into a corner and lay curled up with his back to the room. There was nothing worth staying awake for.

Nathan sat down morosely. Gideon and Abi relapsed into their earlier silence, though Nathan did not feel unwelcome. As he looked round Nathan realised all Joe's clothes and toys had been tidied out of sight. For months Abi hadn't let them be moved. Had she stopped caring now? Abi stirred and Nathan looked at her swelling stomach. Another few weeks and the new child would be born. For some reason the thought infuriated him.

He leant forward and glared at them both. 'It's all right for you. You'll have another baby and you'll forget Joe. But I won't forget. I'll always remember how he used to come to me, and how he liked me picking him up, and how he pulled my hair and – He stopped, horrified that he was going to start crying. Blinking fiercely, he saw that tears were streaming down Abi's face.

Now Gideon was looming over him. 'Shut up, can't you! She's only just getting over it all and you're setting her off again. Think of someone besides yourself for once.' Nathan shrank back, but Abi reached out and pulled Gideon away.

'It's all right, you haven't done any harm. But anyway you're both wrong.' They looked at her, puzzled. 'I'm not getting over it, Gideon; I'm just getting better at coping with it. And Nathan, I couldn't ever forget Joe, however many others I have – though I think maybe Gideon hopes this one will help me forget.' Gideon didn't meet her eyes.

'None of us can forget,' Abi went on, 'though I sometimes wish I could. But somehow we've got to go on, haven't we? There are meals to cook and clothes to mend, and ordinary things to do. That's what we've got to concentrate on now. Not sit around thinking about what happened and wondering why.' Her voice tailed off sadly, and Nathan remembered how lively she had been when she had Joe – and when Mary was just across the street.

'Do you miss Mary?' he asked. Gideon eased his shoulders restlessly. These were things they hadn't talked about before. 'Let's not stir it all up again' he muttered.

Abi smiled at him affectionately. 'It won't leave us in peace until we do. For a long time I didn't want to think about it at all, and I even hated Mary because her son was alive and mine isn't.'

'Don't you hate her now?' Nathan asked.

'No. I can't. She and Joseph have lost their home and all their friends, and they're probably still frightened of what might happen. They didn't ask for any of this – Jesus, and the kings, and the angels and everything.'

Gideon growled. 'Trust your angels to come back into it. The whole town got carried away over nothing. Just forget your angels for once.'

Nathan was stirred at the injustice. 'But they're not our angels. Abi and I didn't even see them – it was you and Josh who told us! Are you saying now there weren't any angels?' Gideon was quiet for a long time and Nathan went cold. Was Gideon going to say there never had been any angels, that it was all made up or a dream? He realised suddenly that he wasn't only missing Joseph and his family, he was missing the hope and the purpose he had known in them. Had it all been a lie? Was everything pointless after all?

'I did see angels,' the voice was firm, but it wasn't Gideon's. Josh had rolled over in the corner and was sitting up, passionate in defending his experience. 'I did see them. We all did. They came from God, and Jesus is his son. We all know that.'

Gideon put his arm gently round Josh's shoulder. 'It's all right, Josh. I know we all saw them, and I remember what they said. But just think about it now. If Jesus was really so special, why didn't the angels come back? Why did Jesus have to go and hide in Egypt? Why did our sons have to die? I tell you what I think. Either God isn't strong enough to help us, or he just doesn't care. Maybe angels are just for looking at, not for doing things. Wouldn't he have sent armies of angels to save Jesus' life, and Joe's, if he could?'

Nathan realised these were the questions he had been pushing away for months. If God couldn't even help Jesus, or if he couldn't be bothered to help, why should they go on? Why not give up now? The oil lamp flickered and almost went out. Darkness slunk in from the corners of the room.

But Abi got up and trimmed the wick. She smiled at them and the shadows retreated a little way. 'Do you remember Joseph telling you about the angels who came to him and Mary before Jesus was born? How the angels gave them a choice? Well, what if God gives everyone a choice? Everyone, including Herod?'

'But God shouldn't,' Nathan protested. 'He shouldn't let people choose wrong. He should stop them.'

'Then what kind of choice would it be? If he gives us choice, it's got to be for real.'

'Even if – if Jesus' life depended on it?'

Abi settled down in her place. 'I don't think Mary would mind me telling you now. You remember when they took Jesus to the Temple, to make the proper sacrifices for a first-born son?' Her listeners nodded. 'Well, when they were in the Temple there were people who knew that Jesus was God's son. They said prayers over him, and one old man spoke to Mary. One of the things he said was that her heart would be broken – pierced with a sword, he said. Mary has known ever since then that there will be unhappiness ahead. She didn't understand it, but she said she would just keep going and trust God.'

'And is that what you're doing?' Nathan demanded. 'Keeping going and trusting God, even if he killed Joe?'

Josh piped up again. 'God didn't kill Joe. Herod's soldiers killed Joe.'

Abi was hesitant. 'I think that's what I'm trying to do. For a long time it didn't make any sense, but this is the only way I can find sense. I know Jesus is special. I think he's God's son, and I think God was pleased when we gave him a home in Bethlehem. I'm not going to forget all that, any more (she smiled at Gideon) than I'm going to forget Joe.'

Gideon smiled back at her with deep affection, and all at once the world felt safer. 'You were wrong too, you know. I didn't want you to have another child because it would help you to forget. I wanted us both to have another child to say to Herod and everyone like him, you can't kill life and you can't kill love. I have a choice too, and I choose not to let savagery have the last word.'

He took Abi's hand. 'I don't know if that's trust, or just blind stubbornness. If you think God had a hand in sending Jesus to us for a while, maybe you're right. But at what cost? I know what it is to lose a son.'

He opened his other hand, and Nathan saw that Gideon had been clutching one of Joe's wooden toys. It was a tiny lamb, small and vulnerable in the shepherd's outstretched hand.

The Baptiser

'The desert shall blossom like the rose.' The words came back to Ben's mind as he watched the camp fire flames flicker, casting long shadows across the spiny, spindly bushes around them. Little sign of roses here now.

'Do you think the desert ever will blossom?' he asked his companions. He should have known better. His words might have been idle, but neither of these two ever left a question until they had completely explored and exhausted it. John's head jerked round and he paused in his laborious shelling of locust seeds.

'The desert blossoms now for people who understand it,' he answered. 'there's food and shelter in plenty for those who know what to look for. And there's a beauty here you'll not find anywhere else – space, a long horizon, time to think.'

Ben grinned to himself. The whole village knew that John was passionate about the desert, and would be off into the empty lands whenever his elderly mother let him go. No-one knew what he saw in it, but he always came back looking deeply satisfied.

Their companion grinned too, but did not stop his whittling. The bit of old branch he had picked up was already recognisable as a spoon. Jesus could never resist a bit of wood – it was obvious that he was destined to be a carpenter.

He squinted along the line of the handle as John finished his passionate praise of the desert, then said quietly,

'Oh yes, it will blossom. The prophet Isaiah knew God, and his words will all come true. But is it all this he meant (a gesture to the wilderness around him) or the desert of human life?'

John leapt back. 'The desert of Jewish life can only blossom when someone puts the Romans in order. They need someone to tell them that being an occupying army doesn't put them above the law. They need challenging to operate fairly, and not take it out of the underdog.'

Jesus shook his head. 'They need more than that. So do our own people. OK, tell them what they should do, but somehow they have to find the power to do it.'

Ben listened as the two of them launched into another of their long discussions. He had never heard anyone else who thought like these two. They treated the whole of Scripture as if it was there for them to work out its meaning for themselves. Goodness knows what the village rabbi would think if he heard them. He taught the boys very patiently, but always admonished them,

'Now remember – scripture is to be revered. For interpretation, I can consult the writings of the learned scribes. Ours not to interpret, but to learn and to reverence.' Not that Rabbi Micaiah had ever heard John in this mood. Sometimes he talked like this to Ben, but mostly he saved it for Jesus.

Ben could remember, years ago, hearing his mother gossiping with a new neighbour. He wasn't paying much attention until she mentioned John, his best friend.

'A lot of very strange goings-on when he was born' she was saying. 'To begin with Elizabeth was a good age, and we'd all given up looking for a child. And then, when they knew John was on the way, Zacharias was struck dumb for months. A heavenly visitation, people said.'

The neighbour was agog 'Were they such bad people, then?'

'On the contrary. He was a priest and they were both the next thing to saints. Mind you, visitations run in that family. Elizabeth's cousin Mary, she met the angel Gabriel, so they say. Certainly she looked a bit other-worldly. She came and stayed with Elizabeth when they were both pregnant. Her son's only six months younger than John.'

'So, is John going to be something out of the ordinary? Maybe he's the Messiah even?'

'I wouldn't think so. I mean, he's quite ordinary really. His parents used to talk about him being a voice in the desert, that was all.'

The words came back to Ben now. Well, John certainly had a voice, and he certainly fitted in the desert. Whenever Jesus came over from Nazareth, the lads would go off camping in the wilderness. They often took Ben – he was John's closest friend when Jesus wasn't around. He couldn't understand half of what they said, but it was interesting listening to people who treated Scripture as if it were alive.

Ben didn't realise how much he valued the friendship until it ended. Elizabeth died, and three days later John called round, a blanket roll on his back and a cooking pot filled with odds and ends in his hand. He was off to the wilderness, and his whole body was tense with the delight in freedom.

Ben couldn't grudge John his freedom, but no-one else could make good the gap. He didn't care that people called him a loner and made remarks about his weed-grown fields and his absence from synagogue. Scripture droned out every Sabbath was flat after John's conversations.

But one day Ben woke up. Or rather Marianne woke him. She smiled at him when he passed her on the way to his field, and for the first time he realised what a beauty she was. It only took Ben a few weeks to decide that here was the answer to his empty life. He washed and shaved, dressed carefully, and made his way to meet Marianne's father at the village gate. His step was confident.

When he returned his step dragged. Marianne was already promised to Nathaniel! He kicked viciously at a nearby stone, but didn't dispel the violence he felt.

As the months passed, his neighbours began to avoid him. The violence in him frightened them. But not enough. Nathaniel didn't see it coming until he collided unexpectedly with Ben in the potter's doorway.

Nathaniel's mouth was still opening in protest when Ben's fist hit him on the jaw. As he stumbled and fell, Ben was on him in a fury of fists and feet, punching and kicking until Nathaniel lay limp. Three neighbours hauled him off and frog-marched him home, mounting a guard on the door overnight.

Next morning a village elder summoned the guards to a meeting. Nathaniel couldn't walk. Ben listened to their brief conversation and knew he had to get out before retribution hit him. He went to Jerusalem, of course. The best place to lose yourself, and plenty of tourists with ready money. There were good pickings for someone who didn't mind what he did.

The years passed. Ben made a good living. But he made no friends, and he found no real rest. He listened to anything that came his way, and one day began to hear rumours about a new prophet, baptising beyond the river Jordan.

'Come and listen' said one of his drinking companions. 'They say he's quite something. Even tells the Romans where to get off. Of course, he's always on about justice and honest living, but you don't have to take that on board.'

Ben didn't think a prophet would have much time for him, but deep within him something ached for the old honesty and the certainties of his youth. He made one of the crowd that left Jerusalem next morning. He would go and see the new prophet, and hear about the kingdom of God.

* 2 *

The way was not difficult to find. Even when they left the main road and turned into the wilderness, the ground was well-trodden. And there was a constant stream of people coming and going. Ben looked at some of them with amazement. Well-to-do men, their belts holding writing tablets and money bags – tax collectors, almost certainly; expensive clothes, which you'd expect from someone who squeezed every last penny out of working men, with a substantial cut for themselves. Nearby a group of Roman soldiers. Beyond them a large family group. And many like himself, with an expression that was an odd mixture of hope and defiance.

The crowd thickened. They were nearly at the river bank. A group of scribes and Pharisees ahead of them had reached the front, when Ben was stopped in his tracks by a penetrating voice.

'Hey! You who call yourselves religious leaders! Who warned you rats to get out of the sinking ship?'

The group exchanged embarrassed glances, and one bolder than the others offered,

'It is true that we are called to lead the children of Abraham..' He got no further.

'Children of Abraham? Don't pride yourselves on that. Jehovah could turn these stones into Abraham's descendants if he wanted. No, you're branches on a doomed tree. If there's no fruit you'll be chopped down, and the axe is poised. There's only one path open – Repent! Change your ways!'

By now Ben was in no doubt, but he slid through to the front of the crowd to make sure. Yes. The new prophet, the Baptiser, was John. Same voice, same message.

Even as he looked, the Baptiser's eyes met his. A great blaze of joyful recognition lit up John's eyes. The two men took a step towards each other, then Ben stopped. John's eyes did not waver.

'Repentance is the only way.' The voice was firm. 'God will fulfil his promises. I am only a forerunner. One is coming who will unloose God's Spirit, and judge all wrongdoing. Free yourself to meet him by abandoning your past deeds now.'

Ben wanted to argue, justify himself, but he couldn't find any words. 'I want to be different' he said. 'What should I do?'

John's arm was round his shoulders. Ben was being swept along to the river's edge.

'Wanting is enough. I will baptise you, to show that all your past has been washed away.'

Still holding him firmly, John dipped Ben beneath the surface of the Jordan. As he emerged feeling unexpectedly lighter of heart, Ben saw that a line of others was waiting to follow him. He stepped aside but John caught his arm.

'Wait until evening. I shall be free then.'

Ben waited and listened, aware again of John's uncompromising courage, and marvelling at the insight he showed into the dark places of many lives. Marvelling too at his patience: whatever the background, John turned away no-one who asked for baptism.

As dusk thickened, the crowds dwindled and departed. Finally only a few remained, gathered round a small fire. John called Ben over to the group 'Come on, it won't be the first time we've sat round a camp fire together.'

The man nearest handed him some bread and honey. 'The bread's from a friend' he said, 'but John can usually track down a bees' comb.' Not a lot had changed.

Ben discovered that these men stayed with John, and drank in his teaching. 'It's not just a matter of changing our ways,' said one, 'this is someone who can help us understand God.'

Ben knew what he meant, and found himself at one with the group. As he wrapped himself in his cloak for the night, he felt happier than he had been in years.

The days fell into a pattern. Ben became used to the constant stream of people coming to hear John, the line of those waiting to be baptised. Then one day he saw in that line another familiar face. He ran to fetch John and brought him at a run. The trio was complete again. Jesus had come to be baptised. Ben was smiling from ear to ear.

But John was not smiling. He stopped dead. Without even a 'hello' he said

'How can I baptise you? it should be the other way round.'

Ben looked from one to the other in perplexity, but Jesus' familiar smile broke out. He didn't say hello either, but answered straightforwardly

'This is the right way.'

Both stood still for a moment, then John nodded and led Jesus to the river. As he lifted Jesus upright again, both paused. Their heads were tilted back and to one side, as if they were looking and listening to something above them.

Finally they turned to leave the water, but Ben saw that something had changed. John stumbled, and Jesus' hand was quickly under his arm to lift him. Jesus himself was walking tall and steadily, with almost a light upon his face.

They stood on the bank.

'Stay for a time?' John asked. 'We could talk...'

Jesus shook his head decisively. 'Not now,' he said. 'Now I need space to think'

The cousins embraced each other, the steam from their clothes mingling in the warm sunlight. Then Jesus set off

– not in the direction of Jerusalem, but away, out into the desert. John stood gazing after him, but Jesus did not look back.

Weeks later, they saw him again. Ben did not intrude on the conversation, which lasted a long time. When they parted, it was with reluctance. As John came back to his group, he turned and pointed

'Look' he said, 'that is God's sacrificial lamb. He will deal with all the world's sin.'

'But you deal with it' Ben protested. John shook his head. 'No' he said. 'I open men's eyes to it, but I can't deal with it. Only God can do that.'

'But how can Jesus...?' Ben's voice tailed off. John looked at him.

'Do you remember when Jesus was baptised? Did you see anything afterwards?' Ben shook his head.

'Jesus and I saw it. A light from heaven, and the dove of God's Spirit. And we heard God's voice, calling Jesus his beloved son. I tell you, Ben' and John lowered his voice in earnestness, 'Jesus – the Jesus we know – is God's son – the Messiah. He is the one I have come to prepare for.'

As day followed day, Ben heard John telling others this, pointing his own disciples on towards the other. He did this with suppressed joy, and Ben could sense a greater freedom in him, like a runner in sight of the finishing tape.

Unfortunately the freedom did not bring greater sense. No-one escaped John's challenge and denunciation, not even Herod, quisling King in Galilee. Ben shivered as he heard John attacking Herod's lifestyle, morals and married life, and was not surprised one day to see a contingent of palace guards in the crowd.

With a sense of foreboding he watched them approach and surround John. Almost before anyone realised, John was being marched away. A few shouts came from well back in the crowd, but no-one risked challenging the soldiers face to face.

Ben did not risk it, either, but he and Simeon, another disciple of John's, followed for miles at a safe distance. They saw John led into the warren of outbuildings at the back of Herod's gaudy palace. For the time being they could get no further. Access to prisoners depended on money for the guards.

Three days later Simeon and Ben met again at the palace. They had scraped together a little money and a little food. The money saw them past a succession of sentries, and finally unlocked a low, solid door. The room inside had no light and little air. They heard the clank of a chain. As their eyes got used to the darkness, they saw him huddled in a corner. The man to whom space and his message had been everything was caged in, with no space and no-one to hear his words. It broke their hearts.

* 3 *

Ben and Simeon cared for John faithfully, but could do little to lift his caged spirits. Even when Jesus moved from Judea to nearby Capernaum they did not leave him, though they sent messages to let Jesus know what had happened. But news kept coming in.

Jesus was speaking to large crowds about God's kingdom. Jesus was healing many invalids. Jesus had restored a young man and a little girl to life. They told John all this, but it did not seem to lighten his gloom.

'Maybe he's grieved that Jesus is attracting the disciples he used to have,' Simeon ventured one day as they left.

Ben shook his head, 'No, that's not him. He wouldn't be envious. But I don't know what he's thinking.'

Next visit he asked John directly, 'What do you think about Jesus?'

John's shoulders sagged. 'He's getting the crowds, but lots of people can do that. If he's the Messiah, he should be doing something more significant, world-shaking. I was so sure once, but now – I just don't know.'

'Shall we go and see for ourselves, and tell you?' Simeon offered. John pondered.

'That might be it,' he said finally. 'Not just to see him, but to take him a message. Ask him, if he is really the one I was looking to, or if I should be looking for someone else? Maybe that will jerk him into Messianic action.'

Ben was less sure, but he would try anything to help John. The two men had no difficulty in finding Jesus; they just followed everyone else, pushing their way through as the crowds thickened. Jesus had a small group round him as they approached, but Andrew recognised Ben and Simeon and made way for them.

Jesus' greeting was to the point. 'How is John?'

'He's sent a message' Ben replied and passed it on, anxious as to how Jesus would receive it. But although his face saddened, he was not offended. 'Stay here' he said.

For the first time Ben realised that they were surrounded by a crowd of disabled people, dependent on sticks, crutches and stretchers. Here and there a thinning in the crowd marked out a leper. Ben was stricken. He had not thought there was so much suffering in the world. But as the sufferers pressed forward there was hope on every face, and as each came to Jesus the hope was realised; sticks were cast aside, stretchers rolled up, expressions of peace replaced grimaces of agony. And Jesus spoke as he worked. Over and over again Ben heard the words, 'faith... peace... God's kingdom...'

After many hours came a gap. Jesus straightened up and turned back to Ben and Simeon.

'Tell John what you have seen – the eyes of the blind are opened, the ears of the deaf are unstopped...' As

Jesus continued, Ben realised that he was quoting from the prophet Isaiah, but that the prophetic words were describing what he had just seen. Ben gulped. Here was he, an ordinary man, seeing prophecy come to life. He looked steadily back at Jesus.

'I will tell him' he promised, 'that the prophet's words are coming true.'

They turned for the journey back. Behind them Jesus was speaking of John's great calling, his unique work. Ben hoped for Jesus' sake that Herod's spies were out of earshot. As they trudged on, they spoke of what they had witnessed, certain that it would fire John's faith as it had theirs, a fire that would see him through imprisonment and execution.

'What will you do next?' Simeon asked. 'Will you go back to Jesus?' Ben shook his head.

'I've another score to settle' he answered. He knew that when John no longer needed him he must return home. To face his village's judgement and Marianne's rejection. To say to Nathaniel 'May I till your fields and work for you, as long as you need me'. And the parched land would be glad, and the wilderness would blossom.

The Informer

Malc's deepest satisfaction was to see people break with no idea that he had caused their misfortune. He knew that many folk felt differently. Baz, chief of the temple security guard, used to revel in seeing fear cross men's faces when he swaggered along the street.

Maybe that was why they were both so good at their respective jobs. Caiaphas valued a security chief whose presence could silence a fermenting courtyard of rowdies. Everyone knew that. No-one knew how much he valued Malc's less conspicuous talents, because very few knew that Malc worked for him.

They both liked it that way, and so did the old man, Annas, who had recruited Malc. No matter that Annas had been replaced as High Priest by his son-in-law, Caiaphas, and no longer had any visible power. He said once to Malc,

'Those idiots think that power means having the chief seat and being on first name terms with Rome. They have no idea that real power is getting what you want without anyone suspecting that you wanted it. You understand that, Malchus, but very few others do.'

That was the nearest to a compliment Malc had ever received. He took out the memory and polished it from time to time, usually when he was polishing his store of coins.

The store was growing, because Caiaphas paid for results, and Malc provided them. Most of the miscreants condemned by the High Priest's court had Malc to thank, did they but know it. He was the one who dogged their steps, recorded their words and their friendships, and analysed everything for the worst possible interpretation. He would present Caïaphas with a gift-wrapped package: dates, statements and witnesses where necessary. Even his victims, tied up by their own words, found it hard to protest.

But tonight Caïaphas was not thinking of past successes.

'Come in' he said curtly 'and tell me what you know about the mad prophet from Nazareth.'

Malc stood motionless, flipping through his mental card-index. Professional pride dictated that he came up with some information, but it would be a waste to offer something now that might be worth money later.

'Jesus bar-Joseph' he stated briefly and precisely. 'A carpenter in Nazareth until eight months ago, when he took to the road. Wanders in Galilee and Judea, may possibly come to Jerusalem for the Passover. A charismatic man whose gifts of speech have brought him a considerable following, more from Capernaum than Nazareth. Has about a dozen regular associates, plus the usual number of women. I could provide a list of names....'

Malc let his voice tail off. The names were already in his mind and could be provided alphabetically, by age or by length of association. But he was getting towards the payment zone, and anyway he wanted to know what Caïaphas was really after.

'Half Judea could tell me that, and anyone with eyes and ears can get me a list.' Caïaphas was ahead of him. 'What I need is a case for treason. No alternative but death.'

Malc was startled. Caïaphas usually dealt in judicial punishment and public humiliation. The few cases that warranted termination went to Baz and his men. Any muttered rumours arising from these incidents readily reinforced Baz's image. Again Caiaphas caught Malc's thoughts.

'Baz is no good to me in this' he said curtly. 'His agents are too well known and I cannot afford public outcry to rebound on me. This needs secrecy.' Malc drew a step nearer.

When he left the palace an hour later, Malc had two bags of silver in the folds of his robe, and a detailed job description in his mind. Retained for up to three years! Surveillance, subversion of any suitable associates, accurate damning evidence. Reporting only to Annas, and only when necessary. There had never been a job like this one.

* 2 *

Annas tapped the scroll with one bony finger.

'This,' he said coldly 'still does not provide what I need. You have spent nearly three years on this assignment. A year ago I made clear that we need evidence to discredit these so-called miracles. You have not provided it. A man born blind, suddenly able to see. A paralytic cured at the Pool of Bethesda. The daughter of a synagogue official, apparently revived from death. These are people whose history can be checked, whose associates are known. Yet you produce nothing I can use.'

Malc could not gainsay Annas. He himself had set off optimistically, convinced it was only a matter of time till he uncovered a deception. The man at Bethesda – a piece of cake. Dozens of witnesses, plus family friends who would surely remember him as a fit man. But all Malc's patient unravelling had reached a dead end. The man had been lying there useless since five years before Jesus was born! Not even the most dedicated conspiracy theorist could believe in a set-up. Every other healing had been the same. Watertight.

Malc hated excuses, and would not offer one himself. Still less would he offer his own opinion, which was that this man actually had some kind of paranormal power. That did not worry Malc; it would just mean a harder fall when the end came.

'There is no evidence for fraud.' he stated. 'Further research in that direction is not justified. Nor is it worth wasting time on the other signs and wonders. Calming storms, feeding a crowd of thousands – all subjective stuff that can't be either proved or disproved. I submit that the best line of approach is to use the man's own words to condemn him.'

He waited. Malc knew that Annas had sent out other agents, prominent men whose task had been to tie Jesus in verbal knots. He watched Annas' features freeze as he recalled the fiascos. Malc had seen them all. A man in the synagogue with a shrivelled hand: men waiting to pounce as Jesus broke the sabbath by curing him, then floored as Jesus asked 'Which is the better way to use the holy day? To do good or evil? To transform life or devastate it?' No-one able to answer, dumb with helpless rage as he went on to heal the man.

Even this week in the temple, the agents had been left silently raging. A long question about marriage in the afterlife – Jesus had no alternative but to either deny the existence of heaven, or make it look ridiculous. Supporters of every possible faction were alert, ready to denounce him whichever way he stepped. And what had he answered? 'You do not understand life after death. It is higher than your theories.'

Annas did not enjoy reminders of failure. 'And are you going to succeed where our legal experts have failed?' His scorn was stinging. Untroubled, Malc pulled out a supplementary scroll from his belt.

Annas' expression remained impassive, but Malc knew that report by heart. It contained enough fire to devour Israel. In the Temple, Jesus had evicted tradesmen, quoting scripture as if he owned it. A whole village of Samaritans gave evidence that he claimed to be God's chosen Messiah. Time and again Jesus had broken the holiness of the Sabbath, deliberately overturning God's law. When he healed a paralysed man, Jesus had claimed to forgive him, a right which only God could hold. And each item was tabulated and accompanied by the names of at least two witnesses, with addresses.

Thinking of the witness detail Malc paused. He went to a lot of trouble to remain unrecognisable, and it always worked. Malc had a large store of clothes in different shades of brown, and his beard could vary from wild and scruffy to trimmed and oiled. Few witnesses even realised that they had given names and homes to the friendly stranger in the well-worn coat. No-one had ever said 'Didn't I see you listening to Jesus last month? Or last week, or last year...'

But Malc's memory turned uncomfortable when he thought of standing in the crowd round Jesus. Never at the front, never at the back. But always, soon after he arrived, he would see Jesus looking in his direction, with a small nod almost of greeting. It could have worried him, but he realised that the man was an accomplished speaker, and tricks like that were part of his repertoire. Probably everyone in the crowd felt that Jesus was talking to them personally.

Now Annas was speaking to him. Grudging acceptance that his material could be effective, could be usable... 'that's if we can get him to trial. An arrest at this time, Passover week, could spark a riot. Or do you have a strategy in mind?'

As it happened, Malc did. The scene came back to him now. A crowd of hangers-on admiring a rich man's hospitality. A woman with hair indecently flowing pushing through the crowd. Incoherent and tearful, she had poured a jar of expensive ointment over Jesus' travel-stained feet. Malc's nose twitched at the memory. Most of the men were annoyed, but Jesus had spoken kindly enough to her. Malc focused not on Jesus or the woman, but on the disciple behind them, who became more edgy and irritable as the meal went on. Afterwards, Malc had walked out close to him, almost accidentally...

'Yes' he said. 'I have a plan in hand'.

* 3 *

It was dark under the trees. The man coming in from the blinding sunlight stood still for a moment, his hand outstretched. After a while his eyes grew used to the gloom and he moved cautiously forward.

'Over here!' Malc called. The new arrival stopped again, then saw Malc under an olive tree and came to join him. He stood with one hand on the tree trunk, his body tense and his joints angular, saying nothing.

Malc appreciated a man who would not be hurried into speech. For a moment they looked at each other, then Malc allowed a small smile to touch his lips. Nothing too extravagant, but a positive indication of welcome.

'I'm glad you could come' he offered. A short pause. 'You and I probably have a lot in common.'

'Such as....?'

'Such as a desire to see our nation reclaim its former glory – achieve its God-given place in the world again.' The tall figure nodded warily. Malc went on without haste.

'For that to happen, we must find the right leader,' another cautious nod 'and also make sure that wrong leaders do not sabotage all that we could achieve.' No nod this time, but the head tilted as if to hear better. Malc continued thoughtfully, as if speaking to himself.

'In a way, the second is even more important. It could be difficult – fatal even – if someone with a sizeable following attracted attention, then made a mess of it. The Romans would crush us all beyond hope of restoration. We owe it to the God of Moses to keep faith, to retain our strength and our role as the Chosen Nation.

'I'll be honest with you, I feel we're in great danger even now. I know you've paid a lot of attention to Jesus of Nazareth. I'm in exactly the same boat. At first I was sure he was the Messiah, and I almost decided to throw in my lot with him. But lately... I'm wondering if I was mistaken. There have been small things, wrong priorities perhaps, that worried me.' His voice rose in a question as he looked up into the other man's eyes. 'But you know him so much better than I do. If I can talk to you it might help me. Perhaps you can tell me my fears are groundless.'

The other looked away, then back at Malc. He let go of the tree and stood with both hands on his hips. Malc did not rush him. Eventually he dropped his hands and spoke.

'I think you're right. Maybe we can help each other. All I'm sure about is that I'm not sure any longer. Talking might help me clear my mind.'

'You've been worrying too?' Malc prompted. 'Maybe about the way he's choosing to support some very odd people. That woman at Bethany, for instance ...'

'That's just it! When he first invited me along it was amazing. Crowds flocking, incredible cures, charismatic speeches. But lately... I wonder if it's all gone to his head. These days he's saying things that are all wrong for the omnipotent Messiah, and as for the people he encourages...'

Malc's hopeful silence opened a path for the man's pent-up doubts and grudges.

'It's not as if I haven't tried to help him. With my business experience I know what works with people. But when I put forward a suggestion he just ignores me! But of course,' belatedly, 'He has chosen me for his inner circle. I owe him some loyalty.'

'You also owe loyalty to your nation. However distasteful it may be personally, we must protect our people. It may be even that we have been called for this very need.' The words echoed powerfully and Malc knew his face was radiant with heroic commitment. His listener quietly dropped to sit alongside Malc under the tree. Malc made room for him, then continued with a fierce gaze.

'The question is, how much do you care? How willing are you to stick out your neck and take risks for the nation? To sacrifice immediate rewards for the ultimate good?'

'I would never be afraid to sacrifice myself in the right cause!' the two men leaned closer together and embarked on a long discussion. Eventually they fell silent, and each heaved a deep sigh. The decision had been made.

'We know where we are then' Malc reflected. 'I am sure that speaking for such a senior and committed follower as yourself, I shall find a hearing at the highest levels – maybe the High Priest himself. When he knows you are willing to transfer Jesus into his personal protection, he will be able to act (and I know this does not matter to you, but I think you will find him ready to express tangible gratitude). The only question is, where to effect the transfer? We are not seeking cheap publicity.'

A ready answer. 'The best place would be here, in Gethsemane. We often come here at night and it's always peaceful and deserted. I could send word when we next set out. Or I could if I knew your name.'

Malc hesitated. His work depended on his anonymity.

'Just ask for the High Priest's servant,' he responded, scrambling to his feet and holding out a friendly hand. 'I'm usually near the porter's room, he will find me.' He did not ask the other man's name. He did not need to.

The disciple shook Malc's hand firmly before he turned and left the garden. His walk was bold now and confident. Judas had got used to the darkness.

* 4 *

To anyone observing the ant heap of the High Priest's palace, Malc was a very small termite. He occupied a room near the gate, cramped and gloomy to discourage visitors, and so obscure that no-one knew if he was there or not. Usually not. Anything he valued was kept in another part of Jerusalem, far more comfortable and secure, but just as anonymous.

But this week Malc was in the palace, stretched out on the grubby mattress on the floor, motionless as if asleep. Hour after hour he listened to the conversations at the gate, waiting through the sound of servants, beggars, guests and tradesmen for one voice. He knew his man would come. The only question was when.

The gate was quiet when he arrived. Most people had gone to eat the Passover with their families that night, so he had the porter's whole attention.

'Your business?' the enquiry was a demand. Malc slid to his feet and oozed out into the shadows. No wonder the porter had accosted Judas – he was huddled so deep into his robes that nothing was visible except two nervously blinking eyes. Malc strode forward confidently.

'It's all right, I know who he's looking for. I'll take him along.' The hand on Judas' shoulder propelled him into the stuffy room. Malc spoke quietly now.

'Is this it?'

Judas nodded. 'Gethsemane. He – they – will be on the way now. They'll stay an hour or so.'

'Wait here. Stay quiet.' Malc sped off to find Baz, already on standby. 'I need a troop. Armed, with torches, but no uniform. Unofficial.'

Baz had done this before. 'They won't mind what they look like as long as they can have some fun. Who are we after?'

'I've got someone to identify the suspect. Bring him back safe, then they can have their fun.' While Baz sent men scurrying with orders, Malc took a bag of coins from the well-guarded money chest. 'One more message. Send someone to tell Caiaphas he may wish to rouse the Sanhedrin council'.

Baz whistled. 'Big fish, eh? It wouldn't be...?' Malc stopped him. 'You don't need to know. Best to say you were just obeying orders.'

He returned to scoop Judas out of his retreat. The hand that accepted the money bag was shaking, but it disappeared into his belt quickly enough. He stared into Malc's face. 'Can I go now?'

Malc's affectionate grip bit into Judas' shoulder. 'No way. Someone needs to point him out to the guards. They wouldn't take any notice of me.' Without waiting for an answer, he swung Judas into line at the back of the noisy troop. 'All you have to do is go up and greet him, so they know who to arrest. It doesn't matter what you say.'

He half carried Judas along the road. The guards' cheerful catcalling echoed back from the Mount of Olives. As they entered the garden, the noise lessened. Steadily Malc pressed Judas forward until they were in the lead. Rounding a clump of olives, they came on a small group of men. One was standing speaking, the others rubbing their eyes as if half asleep.

'Now. Remember, it is for Israel's sake.' Malc gave Judas a push, and the disciple stumbled towards his master.

'Greetings, rabbi.' He offered the ceremonial kiss, then stepped back. The guards surged forward in a mass, and the drowsy watchers scrambled to their feet. Only two men stood motionless. Above the heads of the guards, Jesus' eyes met Malc's.

'He knows me,' thought Malc. 'He knows who I am.' For a moment he felt naked, but Jesus had turned his eyes to Judas.

'A kiss, Judas? To betray me?' Malc wondered if that same recognising gaze was drilling into Judas' conscience. But it didn't matter now. Baz was deploying the guards and four of them had Jesus in a fierce grip, but his calm was unshaken. 'Was it too far to come to arrest me while I was teaching in the Temple? Or was it just too public?'

Malc moved forward to hear better. But the disciples were roused now, and suddenly one of them sprang forward, pulling a sword from his robes and swinging it wildly. The troops, trained in combat, avoided it easily, but Malc ducked too late. A searing pain scorched the side of his head. He raised his right hand. His head was wet, and his ear felt strange. Through streaming blood his fingertips searched, but could find no shape they recognised. Then he located the ear. Almost severed, dangling by a thin shred of flesh. Malc felt sick.

'Stop that!' the order silenced them all. Malc had never heard Baz shout with such authority. Then he realised it was not Baz who had spoken, but Jesus. 'If I choose to call for rescue, a regiment of angels will answer. When will you learn that I am here to do what my Father requires!' His disciples slunk into the shadow of the trees.

The guards stood back too, hesitating, and Jesus approached Malc. He reached out and lifted the severed ear, and his touch on Malc's head was firm and cool. Again their eyes met. As Jesus turned back to the guards, Malc lifted his hand, his fingertips probing. They felt nothing unusual. The ear was just as it had always been. He scoffed at himself; a man of his experience, imagining he had been wounded! Worst of all, drawing attention to himself. He would never live it down.

Then he probed again. His neck was still damp to the touch. His sleeve was sodden wet, red where it had been brown. He *had* been bleeding. From the corner of his eye Malc saw the soldiers looking furtively at him. It was a relief when a muffled command gathered them again round the prisoner.

Now the guards had gone. His work was over. Malc never appeared at court hearings, never confronted a prisoner after arrest. In a few days he would seek an audience with Caiaphas. Payment for services rendered.

But Malc's usual sense of triumph, of power, was missing. He trudged thoughtfully back to the city, reaching up from time to time to finger his right ear. He had intended to go home, but found himself back at the palace. As he entered his room, a shadowy figure leaped at him.

'I did wrong!' Judas shouted. 'You talked me into it, and now it's all too late. He will die, and he could have saved Israel! I betrayed him, and now there's nothing I can do.' Malc staggered as Judas threw something heavy at him. He realised it was the bag of coins and threw it back contemptuously.

'Not my concern. Not my money. Take it back to them if it's on your conscience.' Judas quietened.

'You're right. I will return it to them. I have no use for money any more'. He walked out with an unexpected dignity.

The noise of the palace washed round Malc as he lay on his mattress. Servants running, voices raised in distant argument, a crowd round the fire in the courtyard. He heard none of it, but lay wrestling with something he could not resolve. 'He knew me. He knew all I'd done to bring him down. He recognised me. And he still put back my ear.'

Judas' words echoed in his memory. 'It's all too late. There's nothing I can do now.' That was as true for him as it was for Judas. The night was almost over. Better go home.

He stood up. Left his room. Passed near the cells... he would just check. Baz, on guard outside a door, winked cheerfully. 'They wanted him out of the way while they argued. Not that there's much doubt what will happen. You off now?

'Yes... No.' Malc straightened his shoulders. 'I need a word with the prisoner.'

The Gardener

* 1 *

Jacob had not always been a gardener. In his younger days he had been Joseph's steward, and Rebecca had been cook to the household in Jerusalem. This husband and wife combination suited Joseph. As a member of the Sanhedrin he needed to keep a good household and to entertain on a regular basis. That was why he maintained a house in Jerusalem, as well as his home estate in Arimathea, miles away in the hill country of Ephraim.

Those had been good days. Joseph was a just and generous master. It was said that he was waiting eagerly for the coming Messiah, but Rebecca commented once that for them, the Messiah couldn't bring more than they had. They were happy in their love for each other, skilled and well rewarded in their work, and very deeply content.

It had not lasted. Jacob did not often think now of those grim months, that began with their high expectancy of a child and ended with Rebecca's body an inert heap on the bed. The child died with her.

Jacob knew that he had fallen apart under the sudden burden of grief. The kindness of his friends seemed very distant, and nothing mattered any more. He could not find energy to eat or drink. When Joseph sent for him Jacob haltingly offered his resignation. Joseph sadly accepted, but what happened next was completely unexpected.

'Jacob,' said Joseph, 'I have bought a plot of land. Outside the city. I need someone to tend it and turn it into a garden.'

Town-bred Jacob had never been a gardener and did not want to start now. But he had nothing better in view, and he owed Joseph for his unfailing kindness. One thing led to another, and Jacob was established in the garden.

Not that it looked anything like a garden at first. There were more stones than plants, and a solid outcrop of rock halfway down one side. Worst of all, it was less than a mile from the execution ground on Golgotha. Mercifully, too far to see closely the agonies of the condemned men on their crosses, but the crosses themselves were clear enough. For the first time Jacob saw the rough edge of the Roman occupation.

But it did not come very close. Since he had lost Rebecca, living was anyway a desolate business. And that desolate plot of ground met Jacob's needs better than anything more prosperous could have done. Soon he had built a rough shed in one corner. It held tools, and a plank with blankets which served as his bed.

His sister Sarah complained mutinously at the arrangement. Why live in such bleak surroundings when he had a home with his own relations? But Jacob quietly went his own way, and Sarah resigned herself to it. When he joined them every week for the Sabbath meal, she made sure that he took back enough bread to last until next Sabbath. Jacob had a pitcher of wine in the shed; together the bread and wine met all his need.

The work met his need too. He began by gathering the stones which lay everywhere and used them to lay paths and build a wall round the plot. Then he cleared out the brambles and brought in plants to give shade and hold together the thin soil. Finally he planted olive trees so that Joseph would have some produce and some profit from his garden. As the months and years passed, Jacob's hands grew coarse with the work, but his muscles became strong.

He slowly began to appreciate how much he owed Joseph for the healing this garden had given him. And one day he found something he could offer in return. For the hundredth time he was glowering at the outcrop of rock which disfigured the ground.

'Not fit for any living thing' he growled to himself. Then the possibility dawned... no living thing, true – but maybe a tomb? He knew that Joseph's own family tomb was miles away in Arimathea. Would it not be much more fitting to make Joseph a tomb in Jerusalem – in his beloved garden, a brand new tomb in which he would be the first to lie?

Jacob acquired stone mason's tools and began the work. First he carved deeply down behind the front rock face, separating out a massive stone which would eventually serve to close the tomb. He chiselled out a careful channel so that, large as it was, the rock could move to one side.

Then he began carving out the tomb itself. Behind the low entrance grew a spacious cave, high enough for a man to stand upright. Jacob's hair began to grow grey not just with stone dust but with age, but he stayed determinedly with the work.

Sometimes it was a refuge. When the wind brought him the agonised cries of poor wretches on Golgotha, he would pick up his hammer and chisel and drown them out with fierce noise. By some quirk of the land, however, the tomb as it grew tended to hold and re-echo the cries. They reminded him of Rebecca's last hours, and he slowly came to identify them with Rebecca. All who died, he thought, would be dear to someone. Jacob hammered into the walls his anger at death, his care for those who died without hope and his strong desire for them to find rest. He sometimes felt as if he was building a tomb not for one man only, but for all the sufferers in the world.

The tomb was well under way before Joseph himself saw it. When he did, he was moved beyond speech. But Jacob knew that he was deeply pleased by the way he showed it to his closest friend, Nicodemus. The two of them were now spending more time in the garden, reading the scriptures and talking excitedly. Jacob had a feeling that they were discussing Joseph's long-awaited Messiah, but the thought stirred little interest in him.

Sarah was less reticent. One Sabbath she too told him that the Messiah was on his way. A man called Jesus, from Nazareth in Galilee, with a long list of healings and compelling words to his credit.

'Where did you hear all this?' he asked. Sarah turned pink.

'Well, from Mary of Magdala. You know we've been friends for years,' she said airily.

'You were friends for years' corrected Jacob. 'I thought you fell out ages ago.'

Sarah's flush deepened. 'It's true that we had differences over her lifestyle, but she's changed now. This Jesus has made a lot of difference to her. She's one of his friends.' Jacob's interest stirred. Anyone who could calm Mary's erratic way of life must have something going for him.

But as usual, he let other people's lives flow on without concerning himself. Even the Passover celebrations did not rouse him much, though he faithfully went to share the Passover meal with Sarah and her family. Once more he thought, as he entered the city, how glad he was not to live there now. Every time he went back it seemed more claustrophobic, more oppressive – tonight it felt both fearful and threatening. Jacob shrugged off his imaginings, enjoyed the family meal and went home.

Just before going to sleep he heard muffled noises and went out to identify them. Over on the Mount of Olives there seemed to be a crowd moving. Probably revellers in search of fresh air. The torches they carried flamed wickedly in the wind but cast no real light. Whatever was happening was no threat to Jacob or his garden and he went back inside.

The next day there was more movement, this time on Golgotha. Jacob saw incredulously that three crosses were being erected. The one day between the Passover and the Sabbath – couldn't they have waited till next week? As he listened to the heavy hammer blows and heard the sickening thud of the crosses being dropped into their sockets, he reflected that someone must be in a hurry to dispose of a significant threat.

It was harder to see Golgotha than it had been, and he realised that the day was darkening. The sun disappeared behind thick cloud and, even at midday, gloom thickened the sultry air. Jacob could not settle to anything and found himself just standing, gazing towards the three crosses.

His foreboding became as deep as the surrounding murk. He realised that he was horribly afraid. For years Jacob had lived with despair, but somehow had drawn comfort from the hope of those around him. Now he felt as if the whole world had been plunged into his own despair. Hope was dead. Light was dead. It felt as if God himself was dead.

His only refuge was the tomb. He stumbled there through the darkness and flung himself down.

After many hours, Jacob heard footsteps; men walking slowly and heavily as if carrying a load. As he peered out, Joseph and Nicodemus appeared. Nicodemus had a basket slung over his shoulder, and between them the two were carrying another figure.

They came into the tomb and laid down their burden on the ledge prepared for a body. It was a body. A young man, dead, with deep scratches all round his face like a crazy crown. As they laid him down, the covering cloth slipped and one arm fell out. Jacob looked at the hand silently. There was no mistaking that wound. This man had been crucified.

Joseph's words seemed to echo an old, deep knowledge.

'This is Jesus of Nazareth. We believed that he was the one who would save our people. The Sanhedrin arrested him last night. I want him to have my tomb.'

Jacob understood far more than the words said. In silence the three men began to wrap the body in the grave clothes Nicodemus had brought. They had to work hurriedly as the Sabbath was almost on them, and they could have wept at the hasty job they were doing. But swiftly as they moved, Jacob had time to note all the wounds. Not just the nails, but the marks of a merciless flogging, and a deep spear-thrust in his side. Beneath the dried blood the body was pallid and drained.

They finished just in time, and together strained at the stone outside until it groaned in its channel and fell ponderously into place. The entrance was sealed. The work was accomplished.

* 3 *

Jacob slept fitfully that night and woke before it was light. He wandered restlessly round the garden, unable to relax. The tomb drew him. He surveyed the stone, thinking about the man whose body lay behind it, and felt a fierce pang of loss that he would never know him now.

His thoughts were halted by a most unwelcome sound – the jingling of armour and the barking of a command. As he turned in astonishment and indignation, four men of the Temple Guard appeared, approached the stone and began to fasten a rope cordon round it. The ends of the rope were secured to the rock face and the High Priest's seal affixed at both ends.

Only when this was done did they condescend to look at Jacob. By this time he was boiling with indignation and protested coldly and fiercely at the trespass. The soldiers' glance shifted the responsibility to the officer. He looked Jacob up and down and said off-handedly:

'By order of His Excellency the High Priest, with the authorisation of Pilate. It wouldn't do for anyone to go stealing the body, would it?'

Containing his rage, Jacob counter-attacked 'This garden belongs to Joseph of Arimathea, a senior member of the Sanhedrin. No-one trespasses here, and I will stand surety for any who come to pay their respects.'

The soldiers guffawed and the officer grinned broadly. 'Maybe we wouldn't take so kindly to anyone paying their respects. Where would we be if the body went missing and some unauthorised party began spreading rumours? This one has said some wild enough things in his time.'

'Rumours that he was still alive, you mean?' countered Jacob. 'No way. I saw the body myself. He won't trouble you or anyone again.'

But the officer turned back to his men and after a few final instructions he marched off. The men unpacked food, drink and the inevitable dice. Jacob surveyed them in disgust and turned away. One of them shouted an enquiry about more food, but Jacob ignored him. In no way would he make them welcome.

The day dragged. After eight hours the squad was relieved. The new squad served their eight hours with more backchat and laughter, and lit a fire as darkness fell. Towards the end of the shift they became quieter, and Jacob had the feeling that they were glad to be relieved in their turn. They left the new squad with off-hand warnings and recommendations:

'Remember to stay awake. You never know what a corpse might get up to after dark.'

They went off singing and whistling, but the new squad were much quieter. Jacob realised after a while that the men were glancing over their shoulders at every sound, nervous and unable to get their bearings in the dark garden. He smiled sourly. If nerves quietened their behaviour, he was not going to reassure them.

Eventually a faint lightening in the eastern sky foretold the dawn. A bird sang suddenly and then stopped. Further off another bird called, but fell back into silence. Jacob had always liked the time just before dawn. The garden then was cool, tranquil and full of expectation. He felt again the old expectancy, but somehow keener and sharper than before. Maybe the guards felt it too because their conversation stilled and they stiffened, rigid as on parade with only their eyes moving.

Jacob's sense of anticipation grew. Till suddenly, incredibly, the air exploded round him. The ground shook beneath his feet and a bolt of lightning scorched down to the stone. The fire went out and one of the guards fell in a dead faint.

Then Jacob saw that it was not lightning, but a young man glowing and vibrating with light. With one hand he reached out and effortlessly rolled back the stone. As the light of his presence lit up the recesses of the rock, Jacob saw that the tomb was empty. The remaining guards saw it too and dropped like stones. The young man made no attempt to speak to them but moved towards the stone and sat on it. The light of his being throbbed with almost unbearable intensity, and Jacob wondered if Moses had encountered something like this at the burning bush.

But this was no bush. This was a living creature. Jacob noticed without surprise that the guards, hugging the ground, were crawling as fast as they could into the bushes. Once into shelter, they stood up and ran for their lives. Jacob speculated which would catch up with them first – the ears of the gossips or the spies of the High Priest. Whatever was happening here, Jacob did not think Caiaphas would want it broadcasting.

He realised with a shock that he was still not alone. A small group of women was standing nearby, their eyes fixed on the glowing young man. One of the women seemed familiar, and Jacob realised that it was Mary of Magdala. Her face, like the other women's, was a mixture of awe, hope and bewilderment. Jacob heard one of them murmur 'It is an angel'.

Before they could move, the angel spoke. Authority and tenderness were mingled in his voice, and underlying everything a great dancing joy.

'Do not be afraid' came the words. 'I know who you are looking for – Jesus who was crucified. But he is not here. He is risen, just as he said. Come and see the place where his body lay, and then go and tell his disciples.'

The women had crouched down at his first words, protecting their heads with their hands, but they gathered courage as he spoke and slowly approached the tomb. Bending down, they gazed in for a long time. Jacob heard another voice, this time from inside the tomb.

'Why look for the living among the dead? Remember what he told you – the Son of Man was destined to fall into the hands of evildoers and be crucified, but on the third day he would rise again.'

As the women straightened up, Jacob saw that joy was driving out their despair, and their tears had dried. They began a hurried discussion, and Jacob realised that they were sorting out where each would go to tell the news. He heard Mary say 'I will tell Peter. He desperately needs to know what has happened. John will probably be with him.'

With a few more words the women scattered and hurried off.

Jacob stayed motionless for a long time. He felt like an intruder in someone else's home. The angel looked at him kindly and thoughtfully, but did not speak. His silence was not, however, forbidding, and slowly Jacob moved nearer. He stopped when he could see the rock shelf inside the tomb. At first he had thought it was totally empty, but now he saw that the grave cloths wrapped hastily and grievingly around the body were still there.

For a moment he felt a great relief. Of course the body was there. Of course dead men did not rise. Then he realised that the cloths were lying flat and empty. A little way off was the cloth which Joseph had wrapped round Jesus' head, still in the folds Joseph had used.

Jacob turned away with his mind buzzing furiously. He needed time to think. Then he saw through the trees three figures approaching, two men and a woman. The woman was Mary of Magdala.

On the morning air voices carried clearly and Jacob heard the taller man say with violent emphasis 'I tell you, Mary, it's just not possible. He can't have risen. Dead men don't rise.'

Mary's voice was less joyful and less certain than before, 'But, Peter, the tomb is empty. And the men said he had risen. And after all, didn't Jesus say himself that he would rise?'

The younger man smiled delightedly at this, but Peter cut in. 'Someone has hidden his body' he said shortly. 'All we can do is find out who and where.'

As they came within sight of the tomb the men increased their speed. John reached the tomb first and stood at the doorway, his hand to his side with the effort of running. His eyes devoured the interior. Peter came up a moment or two later, bent down and went right into the tomb. John followed him and they both looked silently around. Without a word to each other, they stooped again and left. Peter's face was heavy with thought, John's transfigured with delight.

Jacob however paid them very little attention. Mary had slowly come back into the garden and with heavy feet approached the tomb. Jacob could now see two angels, one at each end of the shelf where Jesus' body had been. Jacob saw that Mary's eyes were full of tears. It was clear that Peter's doubts had undermined her. The angels spoke to her but she turned listlessly away. Leaving the tomb she stumbled and nearly fell. Jacob ran to help her up.

'Thank you' she gulped as he reached out his hand. Then she scanned his face. 'Who are you? Do I know you?'

Jacob smiled reassuringly. 'I am the gardener,' he answered.

'Ohh' and suddenly tears overwhelmed her. She still made an effort to speak, to ask the vital question.

'If you are the gardener, will you tell me... tell me...' her voice dissolved into tears and she drew her veil over her face. Jacob led her to a nearby seat and settled her on it.

'I will fetch you a cup of wine' he said, 'and then I will answer anything you want to ask me. Is that all right?' She nodded and he moved quietly away. It took only a moment to pour the wine, but when he returned he found that Mary was no longer alone.

A tall man was standing beside her, glowing with strength and well-being. 'Why are you crying?' the stranger was asking. Not troubling to look up, Mary assumed that Jacob had returned.

'Please will you tell me where you have taken his body? I will take it away and care for him myself.'

The stranger answered her with one word.

'Mary' he said. The depth of tenderness in that one name shook Jacob. What must it be like, he wondered, to be loved like that?

Mary heard even more than he did. With a start she looked up. Her face was transfused with joy and she flung herself at her companion's feet, weeping over them and clinging on to him tightly.

Gently he loosened her grasp. 'Don't hang on to me, Mary,' he said warningly. 'I have still to finish the journey back to my Father.'

Obediently she let him go and sat back on her heels, looking up at him adoringly but with a question in the tilt of her head.

'Go and tell the others that you have seen me' he instructed. 'Tell them that I am returning to my Father and my God, who is now their Father and their God.'

For a moment longer Mary sat motionless, then scrambled to her feet. Stooping quickly, she raised one of Jesus' hands to her lips for a moment, then turned and ran lightly off. She did not once look back. How sure of Jesus she must be, thought Jacob, not even to need one further glance.

He realised that somewhere in that encounter he had come to give the man a name. Not 'the stranger' or 'her companion' but unmistakeably 'Jesus'. Two days ago he had handled that body, identified those nail-marked hands, gazed on that face with the marks of tearing thorns. This was the same man. Jacob could not convince himself otherwise.

But he was different. If Jacob had been imagining the scene he would have expected the man to be like the angels, sparkling with light and other-worldly. But this was a human being – fit, energetic, glowing with health and joy, but definitely human. Jacob could see, but he could not understand.

Through his tumultuous thoughts Jacob suddenly realised that Jesus was looking directly at him. He raised his eyes to meet Jesus' regard, and without warning found himself bathed in an awareness and assurance of love such as he had never known. Here was someone who loved him more deeply even than Rebecca had done. The knowledge broke him down. He leaned against a nearby tree trunk and found himself sobbing as he had not done for twenty years; sobbing out all the loneliness and devastation he had known since love died.

Eventually the tears died too, driven out by a bubbling fountain of joy. Jesus was still looking at him. The love was still there, undiminished, but far more. In that steady gaze Jacob found himself recognised and challenged as a man with strength and a future. He felt his head tilting at the same angle of enquiry as Mary's had been. He too was awaiting instructions.

No words came, but suddenly he knew without words that a way was opening before him. He would leave the shelter of his garden and go where lives, not land, were desolate. The knowledge of love that was greater than death would sustain him.

A voice broke in on his thoughts. 'Jacob, Jacob'.

He saw with a start that Jesus was no longer there, but the voice kept on calling, breathless and concerned, and he saw Joseph stumbling towards the garden with more haste and less dignity than he had ever shown. Jacob moved towards him and they met under an olive tree. Joseph's face was a mass of questions. His lips began moving but no words came out.

Jacob was the one who found words. 'The Lord is risen!' he said. The two men looked at each other in astonished joy, and the morning sun flooded them with light.

Week out of Time

Nathan 3

* 1 *

'Joseph!' Nathan stopped drifting with the holiday crowd and began elbowing his way urgently in pursuit of the face he knew. Jostled and elbowed in his turn, he drew some black looks, but made steady progress. Not bad for a man past forty.

Keeping an eye on the half-seen figure, he slowly progressed until with a final effort he could grab the man's shoulder. 'Joseph!' he shouted again and pulled him round. Then his hand dropped in bewilderment. This was Joseph's face, all right, exactly as he had last seen it – and that was the problem. The other man was looking at him with no sign of recognition, which was not surprising. In the thirty years since their parting, Nathan had grown up and aged. Working life and widowhood had turned his beard grey. So why had the other not changed?

'Joseph?' he asked again, uncertainly.

A grin brightened the other man's face. 'Did you know my father?' he asked.

Before Nathan could answer, Joseph's son had grabbed his arm and was fighting his way forward through the crowd. After a few minutes purposeful digging, he caught up with a woman in a grey cloak, and put his free arm round her.

'Don't lose me,' he said, and then, as she looked round, 'here's someone who knew father.'

In the stream of bodies the three of them were an island – or rather a raft, for they were being carried along by it. But the crowd sank into the background as Nathan saw again the familiar smile.

'Mary' he burst out, 'Do you remember me?' and without waiting for an answer he hugged her impetuously. After a moment's uncertainty she hugged him back. 'Nathan? Is it you? After all these years?'

Then she turned to her son.

'James, this is Nathan, who was kind to us when Jesus was born. His nephew is only a bit younger than Jesus.' Then her face set, and she looked back to Nathan. 'Or is he? We heard... about what happened in Bethlehem after we left.'

'It's a long story.' Nathan answered briefly. He would tell Mary about it, but not here, in this dusty overcrowded road. There were things he wanted to ask, too. 'How is Jesus? Is he with you? How did you get on in Egypt?'

'That's a long story too.' Mary looked happy enough, but there was a shadow behind her words. 'We shall meet up with him during the festival. He's with his friends.' She looked at her son with a trace of unexplained anxiety, and James pulled her close.

'He's too high-profile for us this week, but mother wanted to see him. So my brothers are keeping an eye on the business.' For a moment Nathan felt unexpectedly lonely, separate from this family who had once welcomed him in. But before the thought could fester, a surge of crowd movement threatened to separate them. James took a firm hold and steered them to the shelter of a palm tree. 'Hold on!' he called to a group of youngsters who were high up, stripping the branches, 'leave some shade for the rest of us!'

The lads fell out of the tree, surrounded by a shower of branches which they hastily picked up. 'Not for us' one said breathlessly, 'we want to welcome the prophet. Hey, wait for me!' and he ran after his friends into the densest part of the crowd.

Nathan looked, but could see nothing for the thick cloud of dust thrown up by feet on the main highway. He could hear shouting, but the dust muffled that too. Behind him James muttered 'Why don't they use some of that palm to settle the dust? Better than waving the branches like maniacs.'

As if someone had heard him, the dust cleared. The crowd were besieging a man riding on... a small horse? he wondered. James nudged Mary. 'He's on a donkey. Remember the prophet Zephaniah? Do you think he chose it on purpose?'

'No.' Mary murmured. 'Someone else may have thought it would be a help to him. But he's never organised his life to fulfil the prophecies. They just come true round him.' She sounded resigned rather than happy, and Nathan heard a sigh. He looked attentively at the man on the donkey. This had to be Jesus.

Nathan had not admitted even to himself the real reason he had left his son to run the inn at its busiest season, to come to Jerusalem for the Passover festival for the first time ever. Stories of the prophet from Nazareth had run riot in Bethlehem, and Nathan needed to know if this was the child he had cared for, the child accompanied by angels and surrounded by prophecy.

The group drew level with them and Nathan saw a small bunch of men around the donkey. One of them looked up, waved to James and turned to speak to Jesus who was gazing intensely at the yelling crowd. As Jesus looked across to Mary, a smile of pure uncomplicated tenderness lit his face. He smiled and nodded at James, then his eyes met Nathan's. Nathan's unadmitted hope was realised beyond all his expectation. It would not matter now if he never met Jesus again – in that look was recognition, remembrance and ongoing friendship. They still mattered to each other.

The moment passed. Shouting rose in a crescendo: 'Blessed is the man who comes from God!' Others responded, 'Hosanna, Son of David!' Then a group of lavishly dressed men, strutting with all the arrogance of rank, accosted Jesus. Travellers fell back in deference.

The shouting rippled out across the crowd, but in the centre there was a moment of calm.

'Ah,' commented the leader, 'so your followers can be quiet. Would it not be seemly for you to keep them in order, to forbid such unholy extravagance? On a day like this, you should tell them to redirect their energy.'

Jesus looked at the group, then turned in silence to survey the innumerable, shouting faces. He looked up to the cloudless sky, then around at the stony road. The air still seemed to be vibrating with the enthusiastic welcome.

'On a day like this' he answered wryly, 'if the energy were redirected, you would hear the stones shouting.'

He urged the donkey past the immaculate group without another glance. Which was just as well, because the expression on each face was pure hatred.

* 2 *

In the end, Nathan and James ate the Passover together. Nathan had warmed to Joseph's son, and was glad of his company. They met every day of Passover week, doing the usual touristy things, visiting the Temple. A group of Galilean women had come to Jerusalem, and pressed Mary to join them. She had spoken to Nathan only briefly.

'We must have time together, but this week is chaotic. Maybe the day after the Passover we can meet, when things will be calmer?' Nathan was content with the promise. James, he thought, was less happy. He often came back for a meal in the inn where Nathan was staying.

'I had expected you to be more with Jesus and his friends.' Nathan commented. James shook his head.

'I'm not one of his friends, and I'm not sure they would welcome me. There's too much history between us.'

In response to Nathan's unabashed curiosity, James eventually told him more.

'We were fine while the family were growing up. Father died when I was young, you know, and Jesus took over the business and looked after us. He taught us the trade and there was enough work for all of us. He approved my marriage to Rebecca and fixed up good husbands for the girls.

'When we were old enough to cope without him, Jesus put me in charge and went walkabout for a bit. That's when Simon and Andrew and the sons of Zebedee joined him. He wasn't away for long – we all met up at our cousin's wedding in Cana. Odd day, that – something happened about the wine but I'm not sure what. Tasted all right to me.'

'Did he come home after the wedding?'

'Not really. He had a base in Capernaum, but he travelled all over the place. All sorts of rumours drifted in, about him having the gift to heal people. Some of the tales were pretty wild. He came back to Galilee for a while, but he wasn't ploughing the same furrow as us. We couldn't seem to understand each other.

'Anyway, after a year or so it got pretty extreme. We heard talk of death threats. Mother was really agitated, and so the four of us went with her to try and persuade him to come home and forget about it all. But he disowned us! Went on about how his friends were his real family now, because they were helping him do God's will. Well, you can imagine how we felt. We broke off contact, though I think mother sent messages sometimes. His friends don't mix with us and we don't mix with them.'

Nathan couldn't understand. Was Jesus really God's son? If he was, how could he act so callously to his family? James read the distress on his face, and smiled sheepishly.

'It's not as bad now. We've all calmed down and we're on speaking terms again. I guess Jesus just has to stick with what he thinks is right, so we've given up interfering. But Mother worries. That's why I brought her this week, to give her a chance to have time with him. She and the others are eating Passover with him tomorrow, and she's looking forward to that.'

'Not you?'

'No.'

Which was how they came to eat Passover together. When the formal meal was over, they stayed put, still chatting, enjoying the evening's relaxation. Then they heard an urgent voice at the door.

Andrew stood there, dishevelled and out of breath.

'You must come,' he said to James. 'Mary needs you. They've arrested Jesus.'

Nathan didn't try to hold James back, and heard him interrogating Andrew as they strode down the street. Remembering the malice of the Temple leaders, he could work out the answers.

After a sleepless night he went out looking for news. The jostling crowds were all going one way and he went with them to the forecourt of the Governor's residence. Nathan could swear that he'd seen many of these people a few days earlier, greeting Jesus with palm branches. Surely they would support him now? But as he looked from one hard face to another he felt less sure.

Pontius Pilate, Caesar's man in Judea, had allowed the crowds into his courtyard before gauging their ugly mood. Now he looked rattled and on edge, jangling with nerves, less calm than the prisoner in front of him.

Nathan felt sorry for the prisoner. His robes were torn ragged, and what could be seen of his face and manacled arms was covered in blood. A crooked thorn branch had been pressed cruelly down on his head. Suddenly Nathan realised with horror that this was Jesus. What had they done to him in the night?

He could not hear Pilate's voice, but suddenly the governor flung out his arm in a clear appeal to the crowd. The throng around Nathan roared with one voice 'Barabbas!'

Pilate gestured again at the prisoner. Now was the time, thought Nathan. Now they could shout for him and have him set free. He cleared his voice to shout for Jesus, but was overtaken by a tidal wave of sound.

'Crucify him! Crucify him!' To his everlasting shame, Nathan's voice died in his throat. He could not withstand that brutal crowd. Sick with terror and despair, he turned to fight his way out.

That was when he saw James. His face too was twisted by that desperate shame. Neither said a word, but they struggled on side by side until they could turn into a side street. Even then it was difficult to meet each other's eyes. James spoke in a monotone.

'Mother is with the other women. I've told them all to stay indoors, whatever happens. They should be safe enough. Tomorrow is the sabbath, and I'll take her home the day after.'

'Will you be there – this afternoon?'

'NO! I couldn't stand it.'

They dragged their way back to the inn and somehow kept still through the long hours that followed. At one point James said 'I wish – I just wish I could have said goodbye to him.' And later 'It wouldn't have helped him to have us gawping at him.' Outside, the city's voice was a sullen murmur, and even the sun's rays were hidden.

As the daylight faded they both stirred. It must surely be over now. James stood up,

'I must see how Mother is before the sabbath starts'.

But only a few minutes later he came hurtling back, stamping into the house in fury. Nathan looked up in surprise.

'She went to Golgotha! With some of the other women. How could she? I'd told her to stay indoors!'

'That's dreadful. How is she? Where is she now?'

James' eyes blazed with anger as he answered.

'She's with John bar-Zebedee! He was there too. With his last breath my so-called brother handed her into John's care. Called John her son! She's gone back to their lodgings with him and says she will stay there.'

James thumped the wall in his anger. Nathan sat rigid. Shock eclipsed even his horrific imaginings.

Jesus had been the child of promise, the man of power. The one who would transform his nation with new life. And it had all ended in this: shame, condemnation; an agony that had driven him to deny even his own brothers. There was nothing left to hope for.

* 3 *

Nathan virtually imprisoned James. He dreaded to think what might happen if the younger man was loose in Jerusalem in all his churning fury: murder perhaps – probably of John bar-Zebedee. Nathan sent for a meal, which neither of them could eat, then spread another bed next to his own.

By now the anger had drained out of James and he lay motionless, not seeming to notice as evening turned to night. Nathan tried his best to lie quietly too, but found himself tossing restlessly. Every time he looked at James, the other man's eyes were open, staring up at the roof beams.

By the time that day – the Sabbath – dawned, his plan had taken shape. When they both stopped pretending to sleep, he sat up and asked 'What will you do now?' A shrug answered him, but he persevered.

'Are you going up to the Temple today? Or to the synagogue?'

'You must be joking. What has God done for me that I owe Him anything?'

'Right, stay here with me today. Then tomorrow come to Bethlehem for a few days.' He almost added 'Come and meet my family' but stopped just in time. Why rub salt in the wound when James had just lost his brother and perhaps his mother too?

'No.' The tone was indifferent. Nathan took a deep breath.

'Look, Mary must be too upset to know what she's doing at the moment. It won't help if you and John fall out. Give her a few days, then see if she wants to go home.'

It took a lot of arguing, and a lot of silence in between the arguments, but in the end James agreed. There was still silence between them, but it felt warmer.

There was silence outside as well. Few footsteps passed along the street. This was more than the Sabbath quiet; it felt as if the city was under curfew, fearful to move. But Nathan knew he had to move; there was one job that must be done.

'Will you be all right for an hour? I've got to go out.'

James began to shrug again, then looked up. 'Where are you going?'

Nathan swallowed. 'To see Mary. The house is near enough. Let her know what we're doing.'

All James' muscles tensed for a moment, then he unstiffened. With an effort, Nathan thought.

'Yes, let her know. Tell her... oh, you'll know what to say.'

When he arrived at the house, the sight of Mary's tearstained face drove away all words. Nathan simply opened his arms and folded her tightly to himself. There were others in the room, but no-one was talking. He told Mary what they had planned, and she drew a deep breath.

'That is kind of you, Nathan. I don't think James is safe at the moment, and I don't want to lose another son.'

There were things Nathan wanted to ask, but not in front of other people.

'Come with me to the door. See me on my way.'

Outside they stopped. Her white, strained face would have melted even James's heart.

'I think you want to ask me why I came back with John. Why I turned my back on James and the family?'

'I'm not sure I have the right to ask you, but it would help James if he knew.'

Mary gazed at the ground for a moment, marshalling her thoughts, then looked back to Nathan.

'Well, the main thing was that Jesus wanted me to. He was dying and in such pain – and it was the only thing he said to me, so I had to do it.'

Nathan nodded.

'But it goes further back than that. Jesus valued James so much. The two of them were really close when they were growing up. Jesus would come up with an idea and the next thing we knew, James had made it all work. He can organise, and people trust him. I once heard Jesus say to him, 'You are a good man for people to turn to.'

James just laughed and said 'Why would they turn to me when they have you?' But if things had gone differently…' Mary hesitated, 'I think Jesus would have had a place for James. Not to go out teaching, but to hold things together. Anyway, it doesn't make any difference now.'

No, it didn't make any difference now. James did not ask what Mary had said, and the two men spent most of the day and night in silence. Grieving, but glad of each other's company. They were up before dawn the next day, with their belongings rolled up for the journey to Bethlehem. Words came more easily as they walked.

'What sort of place is Bethlehem?' James asked. Nathan began describing the village, the inn, the characters he knew.

'And you say that is where they were when Jesus was born?' Nathan looked at him in surprise. James added, 'They never talked about it, you know. Never said anything about their time in Egypt either.'

Nathan related how Joseph and Mary had come to his inn, and before he realised, had gone on to tell about the angels in the fields.

James suddenly came alive. 'Is this true? Angels from God? When my brother was born? Why didn't they ever talk about it? Tell me everything!'

Nathan hesitated. 'I'm not sure I'm the best person. Gideon saw them, my sister's husband. And of course Mary talked to her about the angels who visited her and your father.'

One look at James told Nathan that this too was news to him. James's step quickened as he hurried to meet these villagers who had known his parents. Then he stopped dead.

'I'd forgotten.' he said. 'Just for a moment, thinking back to Nazareth, I'd forgotten…'

For Nathan too it all came surging back. The pain seemed sharper, now he had remembered their excitement when Jesus was born. How could it have ended like this? How could God have allowed his plans to be thwarted?

James still wanted to hear Gideon and Abigail's stories, and the sharing seemed to ease his grief a little. But the next day, travellers from Jerusalem brought it all back. Nathan heard their story first and took James aside to tell him. James looked at him aghast.

'Still alive? He can't be. The Romans know how to kill people.'

'No, it's more than that. They say he's come back from the dead. He's different – appears and disappears without warning, but he's solid enough when he's there'. Nathan fetched the traveller, who poured out the story to his most attentive audience ever.

'Of course, I haven't seen anything myself. They say it's just his friends and followers who've seen him.' A cynical smile twisted James' mouth, but the traveller gabbled on.

'But I've seen them. Out and about in the city, in the Temple too, looking as if all their dreams had come true at once. Smiling and laughing, walking as if they're going to take wings at any moment. Big groups of them, women too. Not a bit afraid of the Temple rulers or anyone.'

Nathan pressed a coin into the man's hand and let him go. He and James exchanged glances in bewilderment. Nathan struggled to make sense of it.

'We can't just stay here and wonder.' James looked awkwardly at Nathan. 'I must go back to Jerusalem...'

'I'll come with you.' Nathan did not wait to be asked. 'We must find out. It can't be true, but we've got to know.' Half an hour later they were on their way.

The road was busy, but mostly with people going the other way. They had exchanged greetings with several groups going south, before they caught up with one other traveller walking in their direction. Unwilling to be distracted or slowed down, they would have passed with just a nod, but he looked up alertly and called out,

'There aren't many going this way today. Couldn't you make it last week for the Passover?'

James slowed slightly, barely glancing at the man.

'Oh, we made it all right. It would have been better if we hadn't. And if other people had stayed away, too.'

'But you're going back already. It must have been memorable.'

James stopped abruptly and turned on the stranger. Nathan put a warning hand on his arm, but James shook it off.

'Oh yes, it was memorable. The best man I've ever known was betrayed and condemned to death by crucifixion, on trumped-up charges. His family was broken, his friends were flattened and God was mocked. And now there are more trumped-up stories about him being alive. Not that it's any of your business. Goodbye.'

The victim of his anger was unruffled. 'There's a lot you've forgotten to tell me.'

James growled in exasperation. 'If you want all the detail, just ask any street-corner gossip in the city. Don't look at me.'

'James, didn't you pay any attention to Rabbi Simeon's readings from the prophets and the psalms in Nazareth? You were quick enough to remember Zephaniah's words last week. What about all the rest?'

As James stood dumbstruck, Nathan looked at the stranger more closely. Zephaniah – the man on the donkey – the man who had looked at him like an old friend... as his tumbled thoughts fell over each other, that same smile was turned to him again.

'Nathan, you've been a lifelong friend to my family, and it has brought you little but grief. Now, it is time to share the joy.'

At the same moment, James gave a shout they could have heard in Jerusalem.,

'Jesus!' He stepped forward with hands outstretched. All the tears he had denied in the last few days were raining down his cheeks, but under them his face was beaming.

Nathan turned tactfully to look at the Judean hills; he had never noticed before how every stone shone and sparkled in the sun. He could hear the two voices, full of joy and confidence and purpose. When the conversation ceased he looked round. James was grinning from ear to ear.

'Did you recognise him? He's alive! He's broken the power of death! God has been in control all the time, and we didn't realise! I must hurry!' James was almost laughing with excitement, and Nathan began to laugh too.

'What's the hurry? Have you finished talking already?' but as he looked, he saw that the road was empty. 'Shouldn't we wait? Won't he be coming back?'

'Oh yes, he'll be coming back.' James's voice was strong with certainty. 'But I must go home and fetch my brothers. Come with me to Jerusalem first, to celebrate with the others.'

James strode off and Nathan ran to keep up. But he couldn't help looking back to the spot where they had met Jesus. 'In a way I'd like to stay here. I would like to meet him again.'

'No need.' James was definite. 'He can meet us on any road he chooses. And he will.'

Part II

Voices in Advent

Anna

Lord, it has been so long.
Sixty years without him
and not a day
but I wake longing for his smile.
The children were so young when he died:
caring for them gave me purpose
when life was empty.
As they grew they cared for me.
But now my children's children
have their own infants.
I should have gone long since.
What use do my old bones serve?
But that is for you to say.
My place is here
hanging on you as once I hung on him,
growing into your love.
I have little to offer, Lord.
But now and then
I see a fellow worshipper
as you might see him.
His need arrows through me
and you give me words
to challenge or comfort him.
So, Lord, I am yours.
Put me to what you choose.
Maybe one day I shall see
through all the grief
one whose love arrows through me
like the simple love of a child
embracing the world.
But Lord, it has been so long.

Augustus

About time, by Jupiter!
The fools in the Senate
think Empires are held
by flashy heroics on the battlefield.
They begin like that
but what holds them together
is administration.
Numbers, logistics, tax returns.
Soon now it will happen.
The Empire will be counted
and I shall know
population, demographic trends
and tax returns.
Each in his ancestral city
to avoid duplication
or confusion of records.
That ass Quirinius
has raised problems –
his Jews think a census
is irreligious.
I've left him in no doubt,
statistics are the thing
not human foibles.
What difference will it make to history
if a few families trek
from Galilee to Bethlehem?
From this census
comes an Empire that will endure
two thousand years.
And about time.

Herod

I can bide my time.
A puppet, some say,
but climbing the ladder
to serious power.
Front man for the Romans, true,
but still, King of Judea.
One day Rome will outreach herself.
Zealots will rise and clear the land,
appoint a Jewish king.
Myself.
Soon now, maybe
this next census could be the spark
to ignite flaming revolt.
Of course I will stand aloof
while the knives are stabbing
and the swords flailing.
Avoid the firing line
of Roman vengeance.
But when the dust settles
and Jews look for their king
I shall be there
modestly accepting a democratic crown.
All I need meanwhile
is to clear the land
of threatened rivals.
Not difficult
for an organised man
with forces at his disposal.
I shall bide my time.

Astronomer

In the fulness of time
I shall observe and know.
A comet? A new star?
Too early to tell.
Tonight was its first appearance.
I shall check tomorrow.

There are men around
who would read portents here,
who think that all our lives
are echoed in the stars,
or even foretold.
I am a man of science.
I see the stars
follow immutable laws,
ordered, unwavering.
Look at the gods:
hasty, needing to be humoured,
playing with their power.
What god can match
the stars' selfless reliability,
faithful as the seasons,
as sure as sunrise?
What god would bother
putting a star in the sky
to tell us his intentions?
There are no gods.

So I will study the stars
and see where science leads me
in the fulness of time.

Simeon

Will it be today, Lord?
I try not to be impatient,
but ever since I took hold of your promise
I've been looking.
These are troubled times.
Jew, Arab, invading army – all in conflict.
Driven by hate
or by fear.
Do they want to hear
the word of peace?
War is costly
but peace can be costly too.
It means sacrifice
of our cherished plans,
our hopes of security,
of the way we see things.
Only you can answer our need.
Now you have promised
that your chosen one will come in my time.
I shall see him with my own eyes,
your Messiah
who brings peace and a sword.
So every day I go out
looking
at every man in the streets
every tourist through the gates
each worshipper in the Temple.
I know he will come, Lord.
Will it be today?

Voices at the Passion

Judas

Don't look at me like that!
I've watched you this whole week
looking at the sights,
brooding over the city
gazing at the people
with longing yet hesitation.
Remember how you arrived –
the whole crowd acclaiming you
calling out to you
almost worshipping you.
That was our moment.
We all expected
you would declare yourself,
seize power,
dispatch the Romans,
stand revealed as our Messiah.
But you held back.

All week, and you haven't acted.
Something is on your mind.
I see you measuring the people
and it's clear to me
that you need the right moment –
sometimes you look almost fearful
of getting it wrong.
So here I am.
I have created your moment.
Here is force for you to overcome –
call down legions of angels
blaze out your power.

I've got it all set up:
even planned this opportunity
for a quiet word with you
in case you were still uncertain.
I tell you, now is the time!
Declare yourself!
Speak as Messiah!
Don't just stand there,
looking at me
with deep, deep sorrow.

Caiaphas

Don't look at me like that!
Remember where you are.

I am the High Priest
God's chosen one, anointed.
In my hands
lies the future of God's people.
By my contriving
prophecy will be fulfilled.
And you –
rabble-rousing peasant,
dangerous upstart,
will not prevent me.

I alone
once a year
in the Holy of Holies
meet God face to face.
I hold the trust.
The redemption of our people
is in my hands.
I cannot allow
an unplanned intervention
from a rustic ignoramus
to bring us to ruin.
Better far
that one man should die
and the people be saved.

Your fate is sealed –
why not accept it,
show healthy apprehension
or at least respect.
Why are you standing there
upright, unmoved
as if you are judging me?

Peter

Don't look at me like that!
I meant them all, Lord,
my fervent protestations
of unquenchable loyalty.
I would have fought for you –
my sword was there,
drawn at your time of need
yet you rebuked me...
What can be happening?
You, my master,
hustled, humiliated
by jeering soldiers.
And I? without my sword
my courage is gone.
The youngest servant
could have me exposed.
And for what?
What good would it do
for me to die in shame,
abandoned, ridiculed?
What good is it doing
for you to face this ordeal
like a common criminal?

Suddenly, in this courtyard
I remember the time
when you blazed out
'Now get behind me, Satan'
Will you say that again?
That cock crows in my ear
as if I were a worm on his dunghill.
I see what I am,
despise and hate myself.

But you, standing there
facing God knows what,
meet my eyes
with profound compassion.

Pilate

Don't look at me like that!
I know they call you a king
and true, you have the bearing,
but even kings
have faltered before Rome.
Here, I am Caesar
with power of life and death,
and godlike wisdom.
You are right, of course,
my power is by delegation,
but wholly real.
Women are too emotional
(I ignore my wife's nightmares)
I, calmly professional
seek only truth.
Your cause is safe with me...
One moment, please,
while I interview these priests...

As I was saying,
I can sense malefactors –
Barabbas, for instance,
using the National Front
to conceal criminal acts.
I tell you frankly,
I would sooner release you –
just give me some evidence.
Ignore the shouts of the rabble,
I pay them no attention...
unless they report to Caesar...
Come, man, speak up!
How can I defend you
if you won't defend yourself?

The crowd sounds ugly,
the flogging hasn't appeased them...
Your blood is staining my palace:
Hey there – bring me some water,
I need to wash my hands.

Mary

Don't look at me like that!
Your anguish is unbearable
and I cannot ease it.
Your pain burns into my eyes
and sears my being.

But worse still than this death
is the death of all our hopes.
The angel promised so much –
God's spirit in you
saving the sinful world.
But sin has triumphed.

The sword the old man foretold
is piercing my heart
as those iron nails pierce you.
There is no comfort.
Not even those laboured words
squeezed between painful breaths
providing for my care.
I must keep my eyes on you,
not shrink from any pain,
that my love may give you strength.

I must gaze at you
until the merciful point
when your eyes close at last
and you look at me no more...
Dear Lord, I am so tired.
I could sleep for three days.

Centurion

You will look at us no more.
That is a relief.
I hate this messy business
of crucifixion.
I'll see men killed in fair fight
or even the arena
but this stinks.
No wonder the men have drunk
till the wineskins are empty
and they are half stupid.
The feel of nails through flesh
is unforgettable.
Yet you prayed for us,
for our forgiveness
as we hammered you to death.
And when we raised you
with the sickening thud
that jerked your body
on the spike of the nails –
you did not curse us.
So I have stayed sober,
ignored the dice,
to listen
to what you did say.
Words of care for others –
your mother, your friend,
this worthless ruffian here.
Words of trust to your Father
even though you could not find him.

I have seen men die
but no-one has died like you
with a sense of purpose accomplished
and trust unbroken.
God – if there is a God –
is this your son?

Part III

Stories and Voices in Worship

These stories and reflections were written first of all to be used in a framework of worship.

The pages in this section identify relevant readings, give suggestions for hymns and indicate a possible shape for worship. For midweek meetings, one section of a story could be used with a hymn and reading, each week for several weeks.

While most readers will not want to use the stories in this way, it is hoped that this section may give a helpful devotional background.

Say Yes to the Angel

Hymn As with gladness men of old
Prayer
Reading Micah 5, verses 2 and 4
Hymn O little town of Bethlehem
Story 1
Hymn Love came down at Christmas
Prayers of intercession
Story 2
Hymn Cradled in a manger, meanly
Story 3
Reading Luke 2, 1-7
Hymn In the bleak midwinter

The Soldier

Hymn See him lying on a bed of straw
Prayer
Hymn While shepherds watched
Story 1
Prayers of intercession
Hymn Cradled in a manger, meanly
Story 2
Hymn O little town of Bethlehem
Story 3
Reading: Luke 2, 8-20
Hymn   All over the world
           In heavenly love abiding
           Hark the herald angels sing

Death in the Village

Worship for Epiphany

Hymn As with gladness
Prayer
Story 1
Hymn Hail to the Lord's anointed
Story 2
Hymn Meekness and majesty
Story 3
Intercessions
Hymn Judge eternal
Story 4
Reading: Heb 4,14 -16; 5, 7-9; 7,25
Hymn Lead us heavenly father

The Baptiser

Hymn The race that long in darkness pined
Prayer
Hymn   When Jesus came to Jordan
        On Jordan's bank the Baptist's cry
Reading: Isaiah 35, 1-10
Story 1
Hymn The kingdom of God
Story 2
Hymn I hunger and I thirst
Prayers of intercession
Story 3
Reading: John 1, 6-9, 15-18
Hymn Lead us heavenly father lead us

The Informer

Hymn Beneath the cross of Jesus
Prayer
Hymn Come let us sing
(Today is Passion Sunday. One of the benefits of Lent is to give us time to think ahead, so that when Holy Week arrives it does not rush past us with no time to take it in. So today we stop and focus on just some of the events surrounding Jesus' betrayal and death. Of course, the story begins a long time before that. With a man called Malc, who was an informer.)
Story 1
Reading: Mark 8, 22-31
Story 2
Hymn Tell me the stories of Jesus (verses 1-5 only)
Story 3
Intercessions
Hymn Almighty Father who dost give
Story 4
Ps 139, 1-12
Hymn Just as I am

The Gardener
For Passion Sunday or Good Friday

Hymn Hail thou once despised Jesus
Prayer
Reading: Psalm 130
Reading: John 12, 20-32
Hymn Praise to the Holiest
Prayers of intercession
For all who are isolated, rejected, suffering...
Story 1
Hymn When my love to Christ grows weak
Story 2
Silence
Hymn When I survey

The Gardener
For Easter Sunday or after

Hymn Christ the Lord is risen today
        Christ is alive
Prayer
Hymn When Easter to the dark world came
Story 1
Hymn When my love to Christ grows weak
Prayers of intercession
For all bereaved, mourning...
For all who have lost ability to trust...
For all suffering...
Story 2
Hymn Low in the grave he lay
Story 3
Reading: Romans 5, 6-11. Romans 6, 5-11
Hymn This joyful Eastertide

Hymn Saviour blessed saviour
Prayer
Offering
Hymn Tell me the stories of Jesus
Gospel: Mt 12, 46-50
Story 1
Hymn Ride on ride on in majesty
Prayers of Intercession
For those facing death...
Those who risk their lives...
Those who face hostility for their faith...
Story 2
Hymn None other lamb
Story 3
Readings: I Cor 15, 3-7.
Acts 1, 6-14
Hymn Thine be the glory

Voices in Advent

Advent candles

Hymn   Come and see the shining hope
Hark the glad sound

Prayer

Offering

Hymn   Born in the night
Can we by searching

These voices are men and women we read of in the gospel story.

Do any of them remind us of familiar people or circumstances – or of ourselves?

They all speak before the birth of Christ.

What difference will his birth make to their viewpoint?

What would we say to them in the light of our knowledge?

Voice 1 – Anna

We pray for all who are lonely, bereaved, or unhappy, with no hope for the future........

Is 40, 1-11

Hymn   Love came down at Christmas
Thy kingdom come, on bended knee

Voice 2 – Augustus

We pray for administrators and organisers: for civil servants, council workers,

all who run voluntary organisations and relief agencies.....

Voice 3 – Herod

We pray for all who have power over groups and over nations.....

I Tim 6, 11-18

Hymn It came upon the midnight clear
Who would think that what was needed

Voice 4 – Astronomer

We pray for all who seek knowledge, all who research, who learn and who teach.....

Voice 4 – Simeon

We pray for ourselves and for all believers who seek day by day to see the Lord more clearly.......

Hymn Brightest and best
Christ our king before creation

Voices at the Passion

Hymn Beneath the cross of Jesus
Prayers
Hymn Thou didst leave thy throne
Voice 1 – Judas
Voice 2 – Caiaphas
Hymn When my love to Christ grows weak
Voice 3 – Peter
Voice 4 – Pilate
Prayers of confession & intercession:
For all who put barriers between themselves and God
all facing death or the risk of death
all who crucify Christ today by their divisions
all who are experiencing pain, suffering, rejection or loss
of hope.
Hymn Here is love vast as the ocean
Voice 5 – Mary
Voice 6 – Centurion
Finally, the plain account of the gospel writer
Luke 23, 32-46
Hymn When I survey the wondrous cross